NO SHELTER

for
Gertrud Lutzeier
and
Karl Scheuch

NO SHELTER

Elizabeth Lutzeier

CANONGATE · KELPIES

First published 1984 by Blackie & Son Limited
First published in Kelpies 1986

Copyright © 1984 Elizabeth Lutzeier
Cover illustration by Jill Downie

Printed in Great Britain
by Cox & Wyman Ltd, Reading, Berkshire

ISBN 0 86241 129 7

*The publisher acknowledges subsidy
of the Scottish Arts Council
towards publication of this volume.*

CANONGATE PUBLISHING LTD
17 JEFFREY STREET, EDINBURGH EH1 1DR

1

Outside the bombs were whistling and banging like fireworks on New Year's Eve, before they landed with a deafening explosion which shook the houses for miles around. But inside the air raid shelter where Johannes was sitting, keeping a tight grip on their suitcase, it was as quiet and gloomy as a church just before Evensong. Only the glow of a few candles pierced the darkness.

Everybody was sitting respectfully still, waiting and listening. If they did move, they tiptoed noiselessly across to whisper in someone's ear. Johannes looked across at his sister, Kathrin, but his mother shook her head at him and put her finger on her lips. Kathrin was fast asleep on her knee.

Johannes sighed, and slumped down a bit further with his back propped up against the wall. He wished he could be in bed and fast asleep. Kathrin was three now, but she hadn't changed all that much since she was a baby. She could sleep anywhere, whatever was going on around her. She was never afraid of anything.

His mother reached her one free arm round the heavy, sleepy bundle she held on her lap and stroked Johannes' hair. She never gave any sign that she was afraid either. Johannes' mother always seemed to know what to do when the air raid sirens started and she had to hurry them off to the shelter. Johannes was the only one who was afraid. He was often so terrified by the piercing shriek of the air raid sirens, shaking him violently out of his sleep, that his stomach seemed to tie itself in viciously painful knots and his head ached. Sometimes he had to be sick all over the road on the way to the shelter.

But most children had got used to the air raids by now. For two long weeks, from the middle of November to the beginning of December, there had been a bombing raid every night, nights when they had had to rush through the deep snow out of their warm beds and into the cold shelter. If they complained about the cold, their mother always said, "Thank God you've still got warm beds to go back to." It was Christmas Eve, 24th December, and earlier that evening the priest in church had asked them to pray for the poor souls who had no roof over their heads because of the bombings.

Johannes had wondered at first where the people slept when their houses were destroyed by bombs. And then, at the end of the service, the priest had added that if anyone had nowhere to sleep, they were welcome to sleep in the church. Johannes didn't fancy sleeping in a cold church. He was thankful when his mother tucked him up in bed that night. He and Kathrin had even had a piece of gingerbread as a special Christmas treat. And his mother had stroked his head and reassured him, "There won't be any raids tonight. No one would drop bombs on Christmas Eve."

All the same, Johannes' mother had been prepared for the raid when it did come. Her suitcase was already packed with their papers and ration books, some food and extra warm clothes. She had quickly wrapped Kathrin up warmly while Johannes put his heavy overcoat, hat and boots on over his pyjamas. He held his mother's hat ready for her. She always forgot it when she was rushing to get them out of the house, and it was so bitterly cold outside.

As soon as they were outside the house they had seen everybody running and slipping on the icy roads, all with their suitcases and some of them pushing prams, hurrying towards the nearest air raid shelter. Within three minutes of the sirens sounding, trams had screeched to a halt and were emptied of their passengers, and the few cars which were still around were deserted. Everyone had been running and running without a second to lose.

Inside the shelter, everything was calmer. Usually they just had to sit and wait there until the bombing raid was over. They were prepared for it to last for a long time. Sometimes, if bombs were exploding very close to the shelter, everyone had to tie a damp handkerchief over their faces so that they wouldn't be suffocated by the smoke which came pouring in from outside, threatening to drown them.

Johannes had rushed to find a place in the far corner of the shelter, against the wall, and he had kept a place for his mother and sister. There had been a few more minutes of bustling around until people were settled. As they came into the shelter, friends who hadn't seen each other that day had called out, "Merry Christmas!" or they had grumbled about being woken up on Christmas Eve. A man with only one leg who settled himself in the corner near Johannes drew out a bottle of brandy and invited the people around him to take a good swig of Christmas cheer. Some of them drank and chatted, but most of the people in the shelter were absolutely silent, waiting for the bombs to start falling. At that moment, everything seemed to hold its breath.

But Johannes could breathe easily now they were safe inside the shelter. Admittedly, he wasn't able to fall asleep like his little sister, but he could relax and let his mind wander so that he was only vaguely aware, somewhere right at the back of his mind, of the bombs that were falling like rain on Berlin, of babies whimpering in the shelter and of women, quietly, gently singing songs to calm them down. It seemed that these things were all happening somewhere far away from him, while a brighter, more cheerful world was taking over in his imagination.

2

If you had asked Johannes when his father was last home, he couldn't have told you. Not straight off like that. He couldn't have told you what year it was, or what his father had said to him or whether his father was around every day at that time or had come home specially for Christmas. But in his dream he vividly remembered that last Christmas, in 1939, when his father had been there.

Johannes was only four at the time, and Kathrin wasn't even around, as far as he knew. Oh, yes, and Oma and Opa were there too, because Opa had bought the enormous Christmas tree in the market and Johannes remembered helping him to carry it home through the snow, holding onto the tip. Opa had said that was the heaviest part of the tree. And then they had left the tree out in the garden, all bundled up tightly.

Johannes remembered going off to church with his mother and his Oma, just as they did every Christmas Eve. When they got back home, there was a great hustle and bustle because things weren't quite ready. Opa stood resolutely in front of the living-room door, refusing to let anyone in until Johannes' father gave the signal to show that the tree was ready.

Johannes would never forget the sight he saw when they finally opened the door. The Christmas tree, reaching up to the living-room ceiling, seemed to be on fire, but it was ablaze with the candles Opa had attached to the branches. And then there were the painted wooden figures of angels, witches, soldiers, children on sledges and jolly little men in red coats with white beards, and there was tinsel and gingerbread dangling temptingly from every branch.

Before Johannes could reach up to touch the tree, and before he even had time to notice the small pile of presents underneath it, his mother picked him up and took him to sit on her knee at the other side of the room. He had to put up with the terrible suspense while his parents and grandparents insisted on singing a seemingly endless series of Christmas carols. And then they all kissed each other and wished each other "Merry Christmas" and "A Blessed Christmas", and then they kissed all over again. At long last Johannes was left in peace to open his presents and play with them—that is, until his father and grandfather decided they knew better than he did exactly how to play with the toy lorry he had been given.

Yes. That was definitely the last time his father had been there, and the last year they had all had a good time together. But Johannes couldn't have told you what his father looked like then. He just knew that his father was there, that he had carried on stroking Johannes' hair and wishing him "Happy Christmas" when Johannes could hardly wait to get down from his mother's knee and attack the mysterious pile of parcels on the floor under the tree.

His mother kept a photo of his father in her handbag all the time. It showed a black-haired man in an army uniform looking seriously into the distance. His father had sent the photo in one of his letters, but Johannes wasn't at all sure whether the man in the photo was the same person who had crawled round the floor with him on Christmas Day, playing with his toy lorry. He looked far too severe.

After that Christmas, when Johannes was four, his father had been called up to serve in the German army and Johannes hadn't seen him since. First he had been sent to Poland, but now his mother always said he was somewhere in Russia. Sometimes she even told him the names of the places where his father's letters came from, but that didn't mean his father was actually in those places. Even Johannes knew that soldiers weren't allowed to say where they were, in case the enemy got to hear about it and decided to attack them.

Soon after his father had gone, the first bombs had started. Johannes couldn't remember much about that, except that they had all run to the underground stations to shelter, or down into the cellar. Some people had just hidden under their kitchen tables. His mother had told him there weren't many air raid shelters at that time, when the war first started to move in on the cities. Till then, the war had been something which happened far away, in all those foreign countries where the soldiers were.

Johannes wasn't afraid then, at the beginning. He could only remember crying once, when they were running to the shelter, and he had dropped the toy lorry he had got for Christmas. His mother wouldn't let him stop to get it. She had just dragged him along, screaming and struggling, till they got to the shelter. "You shouldn't have brought it with you," she shouted, pulling him along.

When they had reached the safety of the shelter, and Johannes was still howling for his lost toy, his mother was much more sympathetic. "I'm sure we'll find it on the way home," she said. "No one will take it. We can have a really good look for it as soon as the all-clear signal goes off." But they hadn't found the lorry. Two houses near the shelter had been totally demolished by the bombs, their bricks tumbling out onto the road just as Johannes' wooden bricks did when he decided he was tired of building a tower and destroyed the whole thing with one violent kick.

The thing Johannes remembered most vividly from that week when the first bombs came was the funerals. Some people even said that Hitler would be there at the funerals to honour the people who had been killed. Some others said that Goebbels would come. In the event neither of them turned up. There was only the local district mayor at the head of the funeral procession, but it was a splendid sight all the same.

The ten, flower-covered coffins were all in cars driving very slowly while the drums beat a solemn march for the dead. There were a lot of men in uniforms marching along behind the cars, but Johannes was sure his mother would have told him if one of them had been Hitler. Instead, she just said, "Where on earth did they get all those flowers from?" People didn't grow flowers in their gardens any more now there was a war on. They were all supposed to grow as many vegetables as they could.

Johannes remembered it so well because it was the first and last funeral procession he had ever seen. Even now, when there were a lot more bombing raids and a lot more houses getting damaged, you didn't see any funerals.

Perhaps there weren't enough cars because of the petrol rationing, Johannes thought. But then, what did they do with all the bodies? Did they just leave them buried under the rubble when a house collapsed? Johannes didn't know. He had asked his mother once, and she just said, "I'm sure they give them all a decent Christian burial, the poor souls."

"But where?" Johannes wanted to ask. You'd need an enormous graveyard for all those people in all those blocks of flats which had been reduced to smoking heaps of rubble. And the graveyard near their church was very small. The only new graves in the churchyard were of soldiers who had died fighting for Germany at the Front.

Johannes' mother said she supposed that most people found safety in the shelters when their homes were razed to the ground, that they weren't dead after all. "And where do they find to live then, when their houses are bombed?" asked Johannes. But his mother was tired and had had enough of his questions.

When those early bombings didn't stop, an order was

sent out saying that mothers, children and old people were to be evacuated to the country. Oma and Opa refused to leave Berlin.

"Before you know where you are, there'll be strangers moving into the house and taking it over," said Opa, "and the garden would go to ruin if we left. Someone's got to stay here and look after the house and garden. Besides," he'd added, "the war can't last much longer, and what will the boy say then, when he comes home from the fighting to find the house empty, or worse still, full of strangers?" Opa always called Johannes' father "the boy". "No. It's out of the question. Someone's got to stay at home." He looked at Johannes' mother, who was busy helping Oma to bottle the cherries from the two enormous trees in their garden. "But a woman in your condition ought to get out," he said, "and Johannes too. This is no place for children if the bombers keep on coming."

Johannes listened to them while he went on eating from the great pile of cherries he was supposed to be helping to stone. "But what about your safety?" Johannes' mother asked. Oma looked warily at Opa, but he gave a snort of contempt. "No one is going to accuse me of running away from a few British bomber pilots who aren't even old enough to shave yet. They don't know how to fly their planes or what to do with their bombs. You can tell that. Otherwise they wouldn't be dropping bombs on innocent women and children."

Opa's words were bitter, but the cherries were sweet and delicious. Johannes' hands and face were soon covered with sticky red juice.

They were the last cherries Johannes ever ate from the tree in Opa's garden. He and his mother never got to eat any of the ones they had helped to bottle. Only a month later, when she and Johannes were safely removed to the country, a stray bomb, dropped by a pilot on his way home from bombing the main target, exploded onto the garden door at the bottom of the steps leading down into the cellar.

All their winter stores, the jars of cherries and Opa's potatoes were in the cellar. Oma and Opa had taken shelter there as well when the sirens went off in the middle of the night. Opa always refused to go to the public air raid shelters because he said his cellar was strong enough to withstand any bombs the British Air Force could drop on it. The whole place was blown to pieces, and the garden with its cherry trees and Johannes' swing was reduced to charcoal. That was in September 1940.

Johannes' mother was sad enough when she heard the news of their death. But she was saddest of all about it in October, when Johannes' baby sister was born. She called the baby Kathrin, after the grandmother she would never know.

3

They were lucky. Instead of being sent to stay with strangers, as most people were when they were evacuated, Johannes and his mother had been taken in by his mother's distant relatives. Tante Bertha and Onkel Walter lived in a place called Oberdorf, a long, long journey by train and cart from Berlin right down to the south of Germany. Johannes would have much preferred to go to his cousins in Stuttgart, but the British and Americans were dropping bombs on Stuttgart too, and his mother said it was no safer in Stuttgart than in Berlin.

Mind you, Johannes sometimes had his doubts about how safe he was on the farm in Oberdorf. There was one big boy there, a great, long, awkward boy with a red face who delighted in frightening Johannes. He never went to school because, as he himself said, they needed every man they could get to work on the farm. He had an old pair of bull's horns and used to charge at Johannes with them on his head whenever he could get him on his own, bellowing or uttering piercing war whoops. Wolf was his name.

"Shall I take you to see the cows?" he had asked, gently, temptingly, on the day Johannes arrived at the farm, tired out after the two days' journey from Berlin. When Johannes agreed to go with him, he took him by the hand and led him away. He waited until they were inside the barn, then slammed the door shut behind them, so that it was almost totally dark.

His arm was suddenly tight around Johannes' throat. "Got any sweets?" he rasped. "No," said Johannes, truthfully. The arm drew even tighter around his throat. "I don't believe you. Give them here or I'll let the bull out.

14

I'll set the bull on you." His voice was now high-pitched with excitement, and he dragged Johannes along past the row of cows till they got to the bull at the other end of the barn.

Johannes tried to back away, but Wolf kept pushing him nearer to the bull, tied up by a chain which went from the ring in his nose to the wall. "What're you going to give me?" Wolf shook him and pushed him nearer to the bull, who was tossing his head and rattling his chains.

"Has your mother got any fags?" Johannes didn't know what he meant. "Come on." Johannes' eyes were by now used to the gloom and he could see that Wolf's red, freckled face was glowing with sweat. He had large red ears which stuck out from his sandy, Brylcreemed head.

"Come on," he repeated impatiently, shaking Johannes again. "She must keep a few fags in her handbag." "Please," Johannes said. The smell of sweat and the cow dung and Wolf's hand tightly on his collar made him feel faint. "What do you want?" "Cigarettes, you stupid little creep. Take some out of your mum's handbag. Bring them to me, and don't tell anyone, or I'll feed you to the bull."

The door at the opposite end of the barn opened, and a shaft of friendly sunlight fell on the cow nearest the door. "Keep your mouth shut," Wolf hissed, and was gone and Johannes was free to run towards the sunlight. But he couldn't keep his mouth shut. When Tante Bertha held out her great, flowery pinny and caught him in it as he tried to run past her and out of the door, he burst into tears and couldn't be consoled.

His mother was very apologetic about what she called his "temper tantrums", saying that he must be very tired after the long journey. She decided to put him to bed early, in the part of the hay loft where they were to sleep.

"You'll enjoy sleeping up there," said Wolf, who had reappeared in the farm kitchen while they were helping

Tante Bertha to get sheets out for their bed. "There's always a good game of cat and mouse up there—every night. You'll have plenty of rats and mice to keep you company."

For the first few nights Johannes hardly slept at all, but lay awake terrified of the rats, listening to every single noise in the hay loft. It was alive with rustlings, and the scratching of claws on wood. But the cats did their job well. Johannes never saw any mice or rats, and he was soon able to fall asleep without noticing the noises all around him.

Another time, Wolf managed to catch Johannes alone behind the barn near the pigsties. Johannes had gone to feed the enormous rabbits, destined to be made into stews and pies for the family during the winter, and Wolf crept up behind him, grabbing him by both shoulders.

"Aha! What have we here?" he said, in a sinister voice that he had copied from someone else. "An English spy, no doubt. Only one place for a pig of an English spy—in the pigsty." And he picked Johannes up (Wolf was a big strong lad of thirteen) and put him down right in the middle of the mud and straw of the pigsty.

The pigs grunted, but remained fast asleep, lying half-in and half-out of their feeding troughs. Wolf stood there laughing, showing off his great yellow teeth, as Johannes slipped and fell again and again in his efforts to get up and climb out of the filthy sty. Suddenly there was a bugle call, and Wolf saw his friends on the road which went down the hill below the farm.

He set off at a run. "Have fun, English spy!" he shouted, as he raced to join the group of other boys. They were all dressed, like Wolf, in pale khaki shirts and brown trousers, and they marched off smartly down the road like soldiers as soon as Wolf joined them.

They were gone by the time Johannes had managed to

reach the bars at one side of the pigsty and climb over. His mother was furious. "Just when do you think I'm going to have time to do all the extra washing you're creating?" she asked him. "I've got enough to do, without any washing on top of all the rest of my work." Johannes was sent to bed with no supper, too frightened to tell his mother that Wolf was to blame.

His mother did have to work hard on the farm. Even after the baby was born she still had to do her share of the milking and mucking out the cows. And then there was the potato harvest. The farm work still had to be done, even though all the young men from the area had been called up to serve in the army.

The only young man around, apart from Wolf, was the cause of even more work for Johannes' mother. His name was Tom, a great, simple giant of thirty-five, whom even the army didn't want. Johannes' mother was put in charge of him as soon as she arrived on the farm. There had once been talk of sending Tom away to a home because people said he was mad, but his mother, Tante Bertha, had fought against that idea. She had said he was just soft in the head and would never harm a soul. Then she had pointed out how he could make himself useful on the farm, and that had clinched the argument.

Johannes' mother had to take him everywhere, so he wouldn't get lost when he went to do a job in the outlying fields. If there was soup or anything sloppy for dinner, she had to feed him; anything else he ate with his fingers, very slowly, dropping more than he managed to get into his mouth. And when he wanted to go to the toilet, she had to open his trousers for him, just as she had done for Johannes when he was small.

Tom never had much to say. "How'do, son?" was about all he ever managed to Johannes. But he always had a smile for everyone, and Johannes liked him more every day, especially when he was allowed to perch on Tom's shoulders for a ride out to the fields.

And without Tom they would never have managed to get the hay in for the winter. Johannes' mother, Tante Bertha, and Wolf's mother, Tante Sybille, were the only other ones around to help "The Farmer". Johannes knew that his real name was Onkel Walter, but even Tante Bertha called him just "The Farmer".

The Farmer's face was very, very brown and very wrinkled—mostly smile wrinkles—and with a full white beard which made Johannes think of St Nicholas. He was very good at smoking a pipe, and driving the hay carts home and telling everyone else what to do. But he was very, very old, and not strong enough to do the heavy work like tossing the hay bales from the cart up to the hay loft. None of them was strong enough—except for Tom, who would work without stopping until someone told him a meal was ready or until it got so dark that he couldn't see any more.

Kathrin needed a lot of looking after too, because she was so small, and, as Johannes' mother was needed in the fields, it was one of his jobs, when she started crying for food, to take her out to the place where his mother was working so his mother could feed her. When she got a bit bigger and didn't sleep for such a long time, he had to entertain her in her pram, and then, later still, when she could walk, he had to watch over her and make sure she didn't run away and get lost.

His mother complained because there was never enough water to wash Kathrin or her clothes, but The Farmer kept on saying they mustn't waste anything—especially water. So they used the water that potatoes were cooked in to wash clothes. Once a week, on Saturday night, the whole family had a bath—in a large tin bath in front of the oven in the kitchen—and everyone had to use the same bath water.

Johannes was always the last in, after Tante Bertha, Tante Sybille and his mother, followed by the men.

Then on Sunday they all dressed up stiffly in their Sunday best—the men in black suits and the women in black print dresses—and walked several miles across the fields to the church in the village of Oberdorf. The Farmer wouldn't dream of taking the horse and cart out on a Sunday. He used to say that the horses needed their day of rest too. And Tante Bertha wouldn't dream of riding in the mud-spattered hay cart in her Sunday best.

So they walked. To Johannes it seemed an interminably long way, but on the way back, after he had dozed through the church service with his head resting against his mother, he rode home triumphantly on Tom's shoulders.

At least the people living on farms were never short of food in that first year. Tante Bertha, insisting that Johannes and his mother were skinny creatures who needed a good deal of fattening up, used to pile their plates especially high on a Sunday with fat roast pork and enormous dumplings with plenty of gravy.

She seemed to have given up the struggle to fatten up Tante Sybille, her daughter-in-law, who was as stringy and skinny as an old hen. The only fat, round things about her were her eyes which were round and bulbous and staring, like those of a frightened rabbit. Her hair was thin as well as her body. It was a bright carrotty red, but so thin that it hung in lank strands round her head, defiantly straight in spite of her attempts to make it curl.

Her lips were as thin as a worm, but Johannes had never seen a worm thickly coated with bright red lipstick before. Those lips never ceased to fascinate him, tightly pressed together in the middle of her thin, bony, chalk-white face. And Johannes soon learned that she had a thin, frayed, worn-out temper as well, worn out with the nights of waiting for Wolf's father to come home from the pub, and

19

now, with the months of waiting for him to come home from the war. She was sure that the war was a good thing for him because she thought that it would cure him of his drinking for good. And it did.

But meanwhile, at all the mealtimes, Tante Sybille neither ate very much nor said very much. At the end of every meal, Tante Bertha would scrape the left-overs from her plate into the bucket of scraps for the chickens and sigh, accusingly, "You've only picked at it." "It was perfectly adequate," Tante Sybille would reply, and then start to clear the rest of the plates away, with her zipped-up lips so tightly closed that Johannes could hardly see them any more.

It was only very gradually, during that first year at Oberdorf, that rationing became more severe. More and more food produced on the farm had to be sent away to the cities—to help with the war effort, they said. Johannes might not have noticed the rationing, because his mother always made sure he got enough to eat from her plate. But he did notice how, first, Tante Bertha stopped trying to encourage them to eat more and then one day even shouted at Tante Sybille for helping herself to the largest piece of ham.

"It's the men who need meat," she said, whipping the ham away from Tante Sybille and slapping it down again on The Farmer's plate. "How are we going to win this war if we don't keep our menfolk well-fed? We women don't have to do anything. It's them who have the hard time—out there at the Front," (and for some inexplicable reason she pointed with her knife towards the roof) "while we just sit at home and wait for them to win the war for us. It's the men who need feeding, while there's still meat to go round." The Farmer didn't bother arguing with her on that point, and placidly ate his way through any meat which came flying in his direction.

Soon, Tante Bertha was attacking Johannes' mother. "There's no need for you to give them two eggs a week—big, bonny children like that. If you lived in the city, one egg a week is all you'd get for them."

That was when Johannes started "finding" eggs for his mother to give to Kathrin. He would follow one of the hens around when it looked as if it was just about to lay, and then, when no one was looking, put the egg carefully in the pocket of the grey jacket he always wore. His mother was angry with him at first, but she soon stopped shouting at him and accepted his gifts with a shrug of her shoulders and a guilty, conspiratorial smile. They used to boil the eggs when Tante Bertha was out, Johannes keeping watch at the kitchen door in case anyone came. Once Tom saw him as he picked up an egg, still warm, from where the hen had laid it. But Tom gave him a broad smile and put his finger on his lips.

Tante Bertha had responded well to the call, put out on her brand-new radio, to ration food more strictly in aid of the war effort. Later she also responded enthusiastically to a personal appeal by Goebbels for any old worn-out clothes which could be re-spun or re-worked into warm things for the troops in Russia. The German soldiers had gone out to fight in Russia in June, and no one expected that they would still be there when the hard, murderous winter came.

All the generals predicted that they would take Russia by storm in a matter of months. But when the troops were still in Russia in October, their leaders suddenly realised that they would need warm clothes, coats and gloves and scarves, and appeals went out on the radio every day, asking people to give up their surplus clothes.

So when the nights in Oberdorf became too cold and too dark to work outside, everyone sat in the kitchen, the women knitting and Tom and Johannes winding the wool or unravelling old, worn-out pullovers to salvage the wool from them. The Farmer never joined in; he sat smoking his pipe and staring into the fire, and Wolf was never at home in the evenings. If Tante Bertha ever asked where he was, Tante Sybille would just look sourer than ever and say that he took after his father, he did, staying out all night, and that none of her family were like that.

Tante Bertha wasn't satisfied with just sending a few knitted socks and gloves to the soldiers at the Front. Where her son Christian (Tante Sybille's husband) was concerned, no sacrifice was too great—especially when the sacrifice meant giving away someone else's clothes. One day in November, she secretly went through the suitcase Johannes' mother had brought with her, and removed all the things she thought that Johannes' mother wouldn't need any longer—like her best, red wool dress, which Tante Bertha considered totally unsuitable for someone working on a farm. Johannes' mother only discovered it was gone when she wanted to wear it on Christmas Day, because it was her husband's favourite dress.

It was early on Christmas Eve in 1941. Tante Bertha was stuffing an enormous goose, and talking non-stop to Johannes, for the want of anyone better to talk to. "Just think of those poor young lads out there in the cold. Nobody'll be cooking a Christmas goose for them, you can bet. My poor boy! God bless you." These last words she addressed not to Johannes, but to the photo of Onkel Christian on the wall. In his army uniform he looked very handsome, with a beautiful smile, black, curly hair and white teeth.

Johannes thought he looked a bit like Tom, only his eyes were much brighter, not as vacant as Tom's could sometimes be. "You should have heard him playing the horn," continued Tante Bertha, "in the village band—for weddings and that. He always looked lovely in his

22

uniform. And all the girls were after him. He could have had anyone. I never knew why he married her," and she sighed. "He was always a good boy too. It was after he married her that he . . ." Here, Tante Bertha stopped and decided she'd said enough already to a five-year-old boy. After a long silence where the only sounds were those of the goose being banged on the table and the creaking of the cradle, she sighed. "You never know what's coming to you in this life."

Johannes liked looking at the photo of Onkel Christian that Tante Bertha kept gazing at. And he liked the picture next to it as well. It showed a large family standing round the table to say their grace before meals, and, in a wonderful glow of light, with rays of sunshine sticking out like hedgehog spines all over him, stood Jesus, holding out his hands and smiling at the family. Underneath the picture it said, "I am here in the midst of you."

Johannes often looked at the picture at mealtimes, when he didn't want to catch Wolf's eye or watch Tante Sybille's lipstick running with gravy. He was looking at it now, when his mother came into the kitchen, white-faced and shocked. "Someone's stolen some of my clothes," she said.

Tante Bertha carried on stuffing the goose. "Well, I hope you're not accusing anyone in this house. There's no one in this house would do a dreadful thing like that," she said. "So if you've lost any clothes you must have lost them on the way here—when you were changing trains or something. Perhaps you didn't bring everything. It probably got left behind in Berlin and then got blown up when the house did—whatever it is that you've lost."

She was flustered, and went out into the larder to get more onions, but Johannes' mother waited. "I haven't lost anything," she said calmly. "I know what things I brought with me, and some of them just aren't there any more. There's a red dress missing I wanted to wear tomorrow."

Tante Bertha interrupted her. "That was a shameful sort of a thing for a married woman to wear anyway—a mother with two small children, and her husband out suffering in the frozen wastes of Russia. You ought to be ashamed of yourself, wanting to wear a bright-red dress like that. Your dark-blue one is much more suitable for a married woman. And no one needs more than one dress for best at a time like this. We've all got to make sacrifices."

That was the last thing Johannes heard about the red dress. He could see his mother was mad about the dress, but she didn't cry, so she must be behaving. Yes, that was it. When she turned her back on Tante Bertha and Johannes and, without a word, left the warm kitchen to go and sit in the cold hay loft for hours, she must have been behaving. Whenever he was mad about something and cried, she would always say, "Sh! Don't cry. We're only guests here, so we have to behave."

She couldn't have worn the red dress on Christmas Day anyway. That was the black day on which they heard that Onkel Christian had been killed. The letter which came said that he had fought bravely for the Fatherland. It also went on to say that he had been buried near to where he had fallen. It said, "All trains are needed for transporting supplies to the Front, or for taking soldiers home on leave. Unfortunately, none can be spared to reunite the dead with their relatives."

It was a cold and gloomy Christmas Day. Even the kitchen was cold because they weren't going to roast the goose after all till the next day, so the oven was allowed to cool down. The Farmer sat in his usual corner by the oven, smoking his pipe and staring gloomily at nothing, while Tom did his best to comfort his heart-broken mother. Tante Sybille didn't make any noise, but her eyes never stopped streaming with tears and getting redder and redder. Wolf was crying out loud like a baby.

It was horrible. Johannes wanted to tell them all to stop their noise, but instead he went outside into the frozen mud and sludge of the farmyard, kicking stones around until his mother called him in and shouted at him for spoiling his shoes.

"Can't you behave? On a day like this?" she asked, shaking him by both elbows till his teeth rattled. He could see that his mother had been crying too about Onkel Christian. It seemed to Johannes that he was a lot better at what his mother called "behaving" than the adults who were still weeping away in the kitchen. He was never allowed to cry for more than five minutes. After that, they always stopped him with the inevitable words, "A big boy like you shouldn't cry." But they had all been crying for hours, and no one had told them to stop.

By the time the next winter came round—December 1942, when Johannes was seven—things had gradually got much worse for him and his mother and Kathrin. Tom still gave them his warm, friendly smiles, and sometimes even brought them extra food, but the others were indifferent to them—all except Tante Bertha. She seemed to hate them all of a sudden, as if she somehow blamed them because her favourite son had been killed and she had been left with poor, helpless Tom to look after for the rest of her life.

She took to waiting for the postman before he came to the house and hiding the precious letters which came from Johannes' father in Russia. Johannes' mother waited for over two months in vain for news of her husband. Then, one day, she took over Tante Bertha's work inside the house when Tante Bertha was in bed with a bad back.

"Don't bother with dusting or anything," Tante Bertha said. "Just see that the men get fed." But in the afternoon, while Kathrin was asleep, Johannes' mother did do the dusting. Johannes was helping her when she was dusting the pictures on the wall, and three unopened letters fell out from behind the photo of Onkel Christian. That afternoon Johannes saw, for the first time, his mother getting really annoyed with another adult. This time she didn't behave, even though Tante Bertha was sick.

She decided immediately to go to Berlin for Christmas. The last letter from Johannes' father, dated sometime in October, said that lots of the soldiers were expecting to get Christmas leave this year, and that he was looking forward to seeing them all in Berlin, if possible, because he couldn't manage to go all the way down to Oberdorf. He sent them the address of the wife of a friend in his platoon, who could rent out one room to them and let them use her kitchen.

As they were about to leave the farm, Tante Bertha suddenly became very concerned for them. "But you haven't got anyone in Berlin any more," she said. "You'll be among strangers. Why don't you stay here, where it's nice and cosy and you're sure of getting enough to eat? Don't go and leave us!"

"Don't worry. We do know people there," answered Johannes' mother. "I've got my brother-in-law living right at the other end of Berlin, on the south side. I don't think he's got room for us to stay with him, but we might go and visit while we're there. And the lady we are going to stay with sounds nice." "You'll come back soon though, won't you?" insisted Tante Bertha. "Otherwise it's we who'll have to live among strangers. They'll come and check if we've got people staying here, and if we haven't they'll just send us any old Tom, Dick or Harry who's been bombed out of his attic bedroom in the city. Come back, girl. We'll be good to you. Come back to us. And God bless the children, the poor little mites, with that long, long journey ahead of them." They shook hands and kissed Tante Bertha and Tom, as neither of the others were there to say goodbye to them. Then they set off for the station, driven by The Farmer in his cart.

4

At the station, it seemed as if the whole world was on the move. There weren't any trains due for the next hour, but still the platform was swarming with people, all quite prepared to fight to get onto the train, which was the only one that day. Most people were travelling back from the country, where it was still possible to get hold of meat and fresh eggs on the black market, to the city, where it was almost impossible to obtain anything except the meagre allowances they all got through their ration books.

So no one was empty-handed. There were canvas bags and rucksacks filled with potatoes, and suitcases full of hard, dry sausages. There were supposed to be strict controls on the transport of food around the country, but there were just too many people to be controlled. Many were prepared to travel miles to make sure that their families at least got something good to eat for Christmas.

When their train arrived, it seemed to be full already, and people were fighting and struggling to get on, but Johannes' mother shoved him through a window, handed Kathrin and the cases through, and then climbed in herself. Everyone was so desperate to get on a train that there were even men who did the whole journey standing on the step up to the door, and some who hitched a ride on the roof.

Squashed in a corner, clutching his suitcase, Johannes couldn't do anything for the first part of the journey except stare at the man opposite to him, who had wedged a baby's pram in between the two benches, so that Johannes had to keep his legs cramped to the side of it. The hood of the pram was turned towards the man, but when Johannes heard a strange squeak coming from it he bent over to look at the baby.

"Sh! She's asleep," said the man. "Don't disturb her."
But Johannes had already seen what the man was anxious
to avoid letting anyone see.

Inside the pram, snoozing comfortably, exquisitely
dressed in a lace bonnet, and covered with a lacey quilt was
a pig. It was quite unmistakably a pig. The man winked at
Johannes and put his finger on his lips. Johannes winked
back. He wondered how long the pig would stay asleep
and not give the man away to the other passengers, but he
didn't have to wonder for long. The man got out at
Munich, the next station, and the last thing Johannes saw
of him was as he put his finger on his lips and shook his
head to prevent an old lady from peeping in and admiring
his beautiful baby.

The long journey came to an end, at last, and when they
finally arrived at the underground station at Wittenberg
Platz in the centre of Berlin there was a friendly-looking
woman with a mass of black, curly hair, blue eyes and a
round smiling face waiting for them.

"I'm Daniela," she said. "I didn't know when you were
coming, but there aren't that many trains and I thought
you might need help, so I came to meet all of them."
Johannes looked admiringly at the large gold star sewn
onto her coat. He thought it must be something to do with
Christmas. He had seen his Oma making stars out of silver
or gold paper to decorate the windows of their house or to
hang on the Christmas tree.

The walk to Daniela's flat was very short, and as she
showed them the way, carrying Kathrin on her shoulders,
she broke the bad news to them first. "The platoon that
both our husbands are in won't be getting Christmas leave
this year," she said to Johannes' mother. Then, seeing her
disappointment, she went on, "Never mind. We can have a
good Christmas together, and then you can go back to

your friends in the south."

"Oh, no. I'm certainly not going back there," said Johannes' mother very decisively. She seemed to have taken an instant liking to Daniela, and talked to her as if she were an old friend. "The war's bound to be over soon, and we don't want to be so far away when the soldiers start coming home. Anyway, I need a bit of life. I thought I was going to suffocate sometimes, sitting in the farmhouse night after night, knitting, with no sound except the old lady snoring and The Farmer burping." She laughed. Johannes hadn't heard his mother laugh much recently. "You wouldn't believe what they were like," she went on. "Even accused me of being a scarlet woman because I wanted to wear a red dress. Oh, it's good to be back in Berlin, and it makes me feel closer, you know, to what's happening to our men at the Front. It always took a very long time for any news to filter through to Oberdorf—except what came on the radio, and that's not real news. They don't tell you what's really happening. Here in Berlin there's always someone around who's actually been out there, who can tell you what it's like."

She hesitated. "But is it all right with you, Daniela, if we stay in your flat? I mean, we'll pay you rent. We've just got nowhere else to go till it's all over." Johannes hoped it would be all right. He looked up at Daniela as she put the key in her front door. He knew he was going to like her. "Of course you can stay here," she said. "Make yourselves at home." She showed them into the flat. Johannes was at first overwhelmed by the gigantic, high-ceilinged rooms, after the small cramped kitchen where they had sat most of the time in the evenings on the farm.

The first thing Daniela did was to offer them something to eat, some bread and cheese, with no butter. Kathrin, who was too tired to even eat, sat on Daniela's knee sucking her thumb and, with the other hand, tracing patterns round and round the gold star which was sewn onto Daniela's flowered dress. "I'm sorry, it isn't very much," said Daniela. "I only get half rations, you see." "Oh, God, I didn't know that," said Johannes' mother, putting her bread back down on the plate she had just taken it from, "and now we're eating everything you've got. But we've brought some sausages from the farm in our rucksack, and tomorrow we can go out with our ration books and then we can pay you back. I'm really sorry," she kept on saying, and nodded towards the gold star on Daniela's dress. "I didn't know about that either. I thought people who were married to Germans were exempt from all the laws about Jews." "Oh, don't worry about me. I'm very well off," said Daniela. "I shouldn't think anything can happen to me or my family because my husband's German. There are a few things I can't do. I can't have a newspaper, and I can't travel on public transport. But that's nothing. I'm sure it'll all change after the war. They're just emergency measures. Everything will be back to normal one day."

The children loved Daniela, because she never tired of entertaining them, singing them songs while she played the piano for them to dance to, telling them stories, and playing horses on the floor with them. Even though she had a long walk to and from her work every day in a munitions factory she never seemed tired in the way that their mother often was. Once she had worked as a librarian. Johannes thought that was why she knew so many stories. But she wasn't allowed to work there any longer.

Even so, she had a lot of books, more books than Johannes had ever seen. Even Opa and Oma hadn't had so many books. There were enormous books with pictures of flowers, books with beautiful covers but no pictures, books of sheet music which were on shelves beside the piano and, best of all, on the lower shelves, books for children, with plenty of brightly coloured pictures. They had belonged to Daniela's little sister, she said.

When Johannes asked where her little sister was, Daniela told him she was in the East with her parents. Johannes knew that his father was in the East, fighting with the other soldiers, but he was sure that children couldn't go there. His mother had already told him they couldn't go to see his father. "There's a war on there. A war is no place for children." So he asked his mother again why they couldn't be with father in the East, if Daniela's little sister could go there, and his mother had said, "Daniela's family are in a different place. I don't know where. They're just somewhere else."

It seemed to Johannes quite clear that nobody's family was all together. They were all sent away somewhere far apart from each other, all in different places—like Onkel Christian—so Johannes supposed that they all died before they got the chance to come back home again.

Of all Daniela's books, Johannes' favourite was *Hänsel and Gretel*, because of Hänsel looking after his little sister in the story, as Johannes did with Kathrin. Mind you, he never had to look after her very much or face great dangers with her as Hänsel did, but he was convinced he would do anything for her if it was necessary. Even though she was just two, she was the only friend and playmate he had. Johannes had hardly ever known any other children, because there were so few around.

Over and over again he asked Daniela to read him the story of Hänsel and Gretel, and for the first two weeks she was quite happy to do so. But one evening, at the beginning of January in 1943, she suddenly said, at the end of the story, "Right, that's it. That's the last time I'm going to read it for you. A great big boy like you ought to be able to read it himself."

This was when Johannes was already seven. "It's true," his mother said apologetically, "he should have started school last year in Oberdorf, but the school was three-quarters of an hour's walk away. And besides, he was needed to look after Kathrin while I was helping on the farm. Perhaps we can look for a school round here."

Daniela laughed. "You won't find a school in one piece in this area, and anyway, there aren't many teachers who volunteered to stay in Berlin. I can teach him to read, and then he can get through as many books as he wants."

Every evening after that, when Daniela got home from her work, she helped him with his reading. His mother helped him during the day, because she wanted him to begin to write proper notes to his father. But even after he had learned to write, when the writing itself was no longer a problem, he still had the problem of what to say to a father he didn't know. He had completely forgotten what his father looked like, apart from the photo his mother had in her handbag. But the man in that photo was a stranger. So Johannes could only ever write, "Dear Papa, We are all fine. Please come home soon." Except he didn't know whether he actually wanted his father to come home. They had managed very well without him so far.

At the end of February 1943, when they had been in Berlin for over two months and were nicely settled in, Johannes was woken up one morning by a loud banging. Someone was banging violently on the door of Daniela's flat. Johannes and Kathrin slept on a mattress on the floor beside their mother's bed. Johannes looked first at Kathrin, rosy-cheeked and fast asleep. She could sleep through anything. His mother was still asleep too.

The banging carried on. He wondered whether he should wake his mother or just go to the door himself. He didn't know whether it was night-time or already morning. It was still pitch-dark outside. Suddenly he realised that the banging had stopped. Daniela had opened the door, and Johannes heard a brisk, efficient man's voice.

"Show us your papers, please. Everyone has to have their papers ready to show at all times." "Of course," answered Daniela quietly. "I'll just go and get them." "Then I'd better come with you to make sure you don't go out the back window," the man said sharply.

His voice came nearer, along the corridor, as he said this. Johannes' mother was awake. "What is it?" she whispered to Johannes. "I don't know," he said. "A man's come to see Daniela." The man was reading her papers out loud. "Are you the Jewess, Daniela Leah Levy, the person described in these papers?" His voice was formal and solemn, like the priest in church, Johannes thought.

"I have been married for twelve years to Lieutenant Klaus von Beck," she said. "My name is Daniela von Beck." "Your family name is Levy," interrupted the man. "Get your coat, please. You must come with me. Does anyone else live here?" he asked. "No. No one else lives here," answered Daniela calmly. "My husband is fighting at the Front." "Children?" asked the man. "We have no children. It says that in my papers."

Johannes and his mother could hear the man opening all the doors and banging them behind him. He proceeded down the hallway, first into the kitchen, then into the living-room, then the bathroom and Daniela's bedroom and then back again into the living-room, where there were suddenly tremendously loud noises of things crashing and breaking, the piano being banged and hit, drawers being pulled out and thrown onto the floor. They heard the same thing all over again in Daniela's bedroom.

And then the door of the small room where they had been sleeping crashed open. The light went on, blinding them. "Your papers," the man said calmly, with no hint of surprise in his voice at finding that there were after all other people in the flat. Johannes' mother got up to get her handbag with the papers in and put her finger on her lips as she pointed at Kathrin. "Please, let her sleep," she said.

The man inspected their papers quickly. He was fat, and looked tired, with a pale, blotchy, puffy face. He was still out of breath from climbing up the three flights of stairs to Daniela's flat and from rushing round, breaking everything. Johannes realised there was someone else with him, a young, dark-haired man with a uniform on just like the one Wolf always used to wear. He was no older than Wolf either, Johannes decided.

"Where's your mother, lad?" the older man asked Johannes, slyly. "Is she here? Show me where she is." Johannes clung onto his mother. He wanted to cry out, "Mami! Mami!" because he was suddenly so frightened. "He's got very black hair to be your son," said the man to Johannes' mother in the same sly tone of voice. "You're so fair," he said, stroking her hair, which was as blond as Kathrin's. Johannes wanted to bite him or kick him, but he saw the younger soldier watching him, and his mother held him tightly by the shoulders.

All he could do was to shout, as fiercely as he knew how, "Take your hands off my mother!" The older man laughed. "Na! Na! You'll make a brave soldier when you grow up."

Daniela said, very clearly, "I have no children. I told you that." "Very wise of you, not having any children," and the man gave a sarcastic laugh. "We don't want to have even more Jews to take care of."

Daniela went with the men. Johannes, looking out of the window, saw them pushing her into the back of a big van with an opening at the back—like the ones they use to transport horses. There were a lot of people inside, but Daniela was nearest to the back door. She could have looked up and waved goodbye to him.

But she didn't. She was already kissing and hugging some of the people in the van as it drove away, as if she was really glad to see them. Johannes couldn't understand that Daniela didn't even wave goodbye, as she did every morning when she set off for work. He thought she must like the people she was going with much better than she liked him.

Kathrin was still asleep in the bedroom, and Johannes went through the cold flat looking for his mother. He found her in the living-room, crying. She was always crying nowadays, and he did so want to make her happy. He didn't know why she was crying now. Perhaps it was because Daniela hadn't said goodbye, or because the living-room was in such a mess. She had always told them to keep the flat clean and tidy while Daniela was out at work and now it was in a terrible state.

In the living-room, one bookshelf had been totally overturned, with its books spilled out all over the floor, and it looked as if the books from the other shelves had been violently thrown around as well; they were scattered in every corner of the room. There were great gashes in the polished wood of the piano where someone had slashed at it with a knife. A gold-framed mirror had been smashed, and the wedding photograph of Daniela and her husband had first had its glass broken and then been neatly ripped down the middle.

Johannes' mother was sitting sobbing, holding the two halves of the wedding photograph, and she cried even more when Johannes tried to put his arm round her. He said, "Are you crying because she didn't say goodbye? Don't worry. She didn't take any food with her, so now we've got some extra food. We can have plenty to eat today; it's all in a heap on the kitchen table."

His mother shook him away from her, shocking him by her anger, when he had only been trying to comfort her.

Her face was red and blotchy and she looked so old. "I'm crying because she was the only friend we had here," she said, "and now they've taken her away from us, just like they took Daniela's family away from her."

"But why couldn't we have stopped them?" asked Johannes, trying to be helpful. "Why didn't Daniela stop them taking her family away from her?" His mother shrugged her shoulders miserably. "Because they've got weapons and we haven't. That's why," she said.

She stopped crying and started, slowly, like someone sleepwalking, to pick up the books. "I'd better get a brush and sweep up the glass, so you and Kathrin don't cut yourselves," she said in a grey, dejected voice, and went into the kitchen.

By the time it was morning and Kathrin was dancing about demanding something to eat, she seemed better. Johannes was relieved. It had frightened him to see his mother so helpless and sad, crawling around on the floor with hardly enough strength to use the brush. He couldn't imagine what he would do if she was ill, because then there would be no one to look after them now Daniela had gone.

His mother decided that they should stay in Daniela's flat for as long as they could. That was the address Johannes' father had, and if they moved somewhere else letters wouldn't get through to them so easily. There hadn't been a letter since the Christmas one, the one with the photograph in it, but on 1st March another one came.

The letter told them they must try to comfort Daniela as best they could, now that her husband had been killed in the fighting. It was obvious that Johannes' father thought that Daniela had already received the news of her husband's death. "Shall we write and tell her?" asked Johannes. His mother's answer was strange. "I don't think we're allowed to write letters to her," she said. "I don't think they'd like us to ask where she's gone."

5

The next night left them with no time to think about
Daniela: the night sky was lit up brilliantly by the
fireworks of the first big bombing raid since they had been
back in Berlin. They were lucky that there was an air raid
shelter not far from their house. They seemed to be lucky
all the time. In the air raid shelter, an old lady gave both of
the children bread and jam.

Johannes and Kathrin didn't ask her how she came by it.
They were always hungry and grateful for anything anyone
gave them to eat. But their mother gave the old lady a
surprised, questioning look. It was almost impossible to
get hold of jam or the sugar to make it at that time.

"Oooh, don't you go looking at me like that," said the
old lady. "I didn't steal it. I've had that jam in the cellar
since I made a whole pile last year. And I thought well, if
the British bombers are going to come and blow all our
houses to bits like they say, well, stands to reason. I may as
well eat it now, enjoy it while I still can."

She leaned over closer to Johannes' mother, tapping her
on the arm as she said, "And I'd rather give it away to
lovely German children like yours than have it fall into
enemy hands, if there's an invasion that is. I'd break all
my pots of jam and set fire to everything myself, rather
than have it falling into enemy hands!" Her voice got
louder, and she looked wildly all around her, as if to
reassure herself that there was no enemy lurking in the air
raid shelter ready to steal her jam. Johannes' mother
calmed her down. "Sh! Don't worry, there won't be an
invasion. My husband's a soldier out at the Front, and he
says they're confident of victory in a matter of months.

There's no question of an invasion." The old lady was quiet after that.

And then, when the raid was over and the British bombers had gone, they were safe and their house was almost in one piece. The only damage was to the kitchen window, which had been blown out by the blast from a bomb falling on the house behind theirs. There was no question of them going straight home though. Johannes' mother had to help with the slow, sad work of trying to dig out the people who were wounded or dead and buried under the mountains of rubble from houses demolished by the bombings. Johannes stood watching the rescue workers, and watching over Kathrin, asleep in the pram that someone from church had given them.

It was freezing, and Johannes' toes were wet and numb with chilblains. Dawn broke, not the clear blue sky you normally get on one of those crisp, frosty mornings at the beginning of March, but to foul smells and yellow, filthy smoke, to the sight of broken crockery and books strewn over what had once been the road. Houses were stripped of their roofs, or had whole walls ripped away.

A woman, whom Johannes recognised as being from the house next door, was walking up and down in front of the ruins of the house, wrapped only in a tartan blanket over her night-gown. Bare feet she had. Her feet were wet and red and dirty, but her face was white and frightened, and she was crying out loud, like a frightened child. Johannes looked in amazement at her straggly grey locks of hair, which were normally carefully, severely plaited on top of her head. He stared at her ashen, grey, tearful face and thought, she doesn't seem to realise how cold it is.

"Aren't you cold?" he asked her, the next time her restless pacing up and down brought her near him, but she didn't seem to notice what he said, so loudly was she crying. She was the only person making a noise.

38

The streets were full of people, but they were all quiet, listening every five minutes for any signs of life which might come from somewhere underneath the masses of brick and plaster, wooden beams and broken furniture. Nobody had any respect for property at that moment. In their search for survivors, clothes, odd shoes and pictures were just pitched onto the pavement while the people carried on working feverishly.

Only the bodies they found were still treated with some respect, covered up if there was any covering to be had, till a lorry came to take them away. Johannes' mother tried to keep him away from the place where she was working with some other women because a whole house with twenty flats in it had collapsed, burying the people who had taken shelter in the cellar.

She had made him stand on the opposite side of the road with Kathrin, but he was still able to see them bringing the people out. Some of them were dead with their eyes open, some with their arms flung out or their legs bent up, but they were already so stiff that it was impossible for the people who unearthed them to straighten their tortured limbs. They made strange horrid shapes under the blankets which were thrown over them, so that Johannes had nightmares for months afterwards about the people under the blankets, some with blood on their clothes and their faces and some looking as clean and peaceful as though they were asleep.

The lady in the tartan blanket walked up and looked at them, mumbling silently to herself, as they were being carried to the lorry. Then she picked up two broken coat-hangers from the pavement, and clutching them tightly to her breast, resumed her restless walking, up and down, up and down. Finally, someone came and led her away to an ambulance.

Johannes was surprised that she was being taken away in

an ambulance, because he hadn't noticed that she had hurt herself. There was no blood, so she hadn't cut herself, and she was certainly able to walk, so she couldn't have broken anything. "Frau Schwarz isn't hurt, is she?" he said to his mother. She watched the thin, weary old woman being helped into the ambulance and then said, "Frau Schwarz needs someone to look after her, that's all. She doesn't take care of herself properly."

At about nine o'clock in the morning, they brought round bread and thin, watery soup for the rescue workers. Johannes could see that his mother was exhausted and grateful for the rest. But she wasn't hungry at all. She took the soup from the woman in uniform who was doling it out, and then gave it to the children, telling Johannes to take his to the other side of the road.

"You'll all get get 50 grammes more meat this week," said the soup woman, with a broad, benevolent smile. "There's always an extra 50 grammes after an air raid. Now that's something to look forward to, isn't it? And ten extra cigarettes. But I don't suppose you smoke, do you dear?" She smiled and looked keenly at Johannes' mother, who shook her head. "No, I never have done."

"Oooh! You shouldn't have said that," said the woman behind her in the queue. "You should just take the cigarettes and then swop 'em for something better, something to eat, or something nice to wear. You can always get what you want if you've got enough cigarettes to give in exchange. Don't you go turning cigarettes down again, love. You can always give 'em to me, you know!" The woman sat down next to Johannes' mother, on a broken wall, and hurriedly gobbled her soup.

Johannes decided to go back to their flat with Kathrin. Since she had woken up, she had been hopping about all over the road, choosing a brick to climb onto and then proudly jumping off it again over and over, till she fell and had to be comforted. Sometimes she banged with a spoon she had found, on bricks, on wood, or on pieces of broken china. She was wrapped up in her red woollen pixie hood and the heavy grey coat they had given her in Oberdorf, and Johannes was kept warm enough running around after her, to make sure she didn't fall down a hole.

"We've got Hitler to thank for this," said the woman from the queue, who had started working again near Johannes' mother. Johannes' mother looked nervously over towards the soldiers who were digging near to where another cellar entrance had caved in. "It's better not to say things like that so loudly," she said gently.

The woman laughed bitterly. "That's what people said to us in Cologne. When our house was burned down by the British bombers, and my son, home on leave, was buried in the cellar, they said we'd better keep quiet about it. Why, I even had to sign a form, before they gave me my flat here and my job in the munitions factory. I had to sign a form saying I wouldn't talk about what happened that night in Cologne. But you can only take so much. I don't care what I say or who hears me any longer. When you've lost your home and your family—everyone you ever had—what more can they take from you?"

She pointed with her thumb towards the soldiers as she said this, but they were too busy digging to notice what she was saying. "The whole German army ought to be lined up against a wall and shot—and Hitler ought to be shot ten times. Then perhaps the British and Americans would stop dropping bombs on women and children. That's what I think. That night when they dropped the bombs on Cologne at the end of May, it was Hell on earth, I can tell you. Last night was nothing, compared to what it was like in Cologne. Here in Berlin, there's a few houses still standing—like that one over there, where I live. In Cologne, everything was flattened." The house she had

41

pointed to was the one where Daniela's flat was as well. Evi Schulz was the woman's name. She lived alone, in one room on the ground floor.

Johannes' mother suddenly noticed that he was still there, listening to Evi. She knew it was dangerous for him to hear such disrespectful talk about Hitler and the army, so she told him to go into the house. "Kathrin will get cold," she said, "and it's far too dangerous out here. There's so much for her to cut herself on."

Evi looked surprised and then shocked when she saw who the children belonged to. "Oooh! Sorry, love. I've been saying the wrong things again, 'aven't I? You look so young, I didn't think you'd be married with a couple of kids. And what's the betting you're a widow, with a husband who gave his life for the Fatherland? If your husband's been killed out there at the Front, I shouldn't have said all those things about the army being all rotten. They say we're all supposed to work together and not go criticising the army, but . . ."

"Oh, no, my husband hasn't been killed," interrupted Johannes' mother. "He's coming home very soon on leave. You'll be able to seem him when he comes home." "When are you expecting him?" asked Evi sceptically. Johannes was listening again, holding tight to Kathrin's hand to stop her running away.

"The last letter we had was dated December," said his mother, "and then he told us to expect him for the middle of March." "Where is he?" asked Evi, this time even more dubiously. "In the East," answered Johannes' mother. Evi shook her head and looked at them, all three of them, full of pity. "That lot won't be home for a long time," she said. Then she bent closer to Johannes' mother and lowered her voice. "I heard someone say they'd surrendered to the Russians and if that's true . . ." She made a choking noise as she ran her finger across her throat.

Johannes' mother looked up, caught sight of him and Kathrin and screeched at them angrily, "I thought I told you to go back to the flat." She turned back to her work and looked up only one more time, to shout at them again, "Go home. Didn't you hear what I said? Go home!"

She came home, tired and dejected, in the afternoon. Johannes and Kathrin were both in her bed, looking at books, because the flat was so cold. Soon she had some hot camomile tea ready to warm them up, and a piece of bread for each of them.

By evening the house was full of strange people who had been made homeless in the bombings the night before. In the whole of Berlin, 35,000 people had lost their homes. Five of them were sent to stay in the flat with Johannes and his mother and Kathrin, though they were allowed to keep the bedroom just for the three of them. Johannes quickly made sure he removed all his favourite books from the living-room before a family moved in there—an old man and woman with their five-year-old granddaughter. A young woman and a baby were to move into Daniela's bedroom. Kathrin was thrilled when the baby arrived. In fact all of them, complete strangers as they were, were happy enough to be squashed together in one flat. In the bombings the night before, 711 people had been killed, and 1,570 wounded. The people who had only lost their houses were among the lucky ones.

6

For almost the whole of the rest of the year, the house was full of life and full of children. Most of Berlin's children were supposed to have been evacuated to the country, but, slowly but surely, they all came drifting back. Parents didn't want to be separated for so long from their children, and people who were used to life in the big city just couldn't settle down to life in the country.

If there was one thing Kathrin was good at, it was making friends, not only with the children, but with the adults as well. She soon learned to run up and down the winding stairs of the house, and she learned which flats she was likely to get a friendly reception at when she rang loudly at their doorbells.

The bells were usually so high up that once she had managed to reach the bell-pull, she hung onto it for dear life, letting the bell ring and ring until someone opened and said, "Hallo, you little witch. Are you trying to waken the dead?" Everyone in the house was fond of Kathrin because she was so friendly and always had a smile for them.

Even the two old ladies who lived right on the top floor, and who were more disgruntled than usual, on account of having three homeless people billeted on them, never had a cross word for Kathrin. When their doorbell rang, they would usually open it a tiny crack and then shut it again, but for Kathrin they would leave it wide open.

They let her have the run of their store of toys too. Nobody could buy new toys at that time. Just before Christmas, old, familiar toys would disappear, and then reappear on Christmas day with a fresh coat of paint, but there was rarely anything new. The books which Daniela had given him had been Johannes' presents that Christmas. But when Kathrin made friends with the two old ladies, she gained access to a whole wonderland of toys which Johannes would never have found on his own because he was far too shy.

For a start, he needed the excuse of looking after Kathrin (though she was quite capable of looking after herself), before he could pluck up courage even to talk to new, strange people, let alone go into their houses. He was, always had been, like a frightened rabbit, turning tail and running back to his mother if anyone so much as spoke to him. But Kathrin was never frightened.

Why should she be, when people were always so nice to her, always pleased to see her? Patting her blond, curly hair, they would say, "Come on in, little witch, and we'll see what we can find for you to play with." And Johannes always went along with her, as her protector.

The old ladies who lived upstairs seemed to understand Johannes' shyness better than anyone. Though they made a fuss of Kathrin, helping her to dress and undress dolls, they used to leave him alone in the nursery. It was still full of the toys they had shared with their younger brother, years before. They were very proud of their brother who was a general, fighting in France. They were only sorry that he had never married, so that they couldn't pass the toys on to his children.

Johannes played for hours on his own with a model shop, which had a shopkeeper about a foot high, miniature scales on the counter and tiny copies of packets and tins of food—some which Johannes remembered seeing before, in the real shops, and some which he had never seen. There were even tiny brown paper bags, marked A. Goodchild & Co., and potatoes, cheeses, hams and apples made of plaster and stuck to the plates.

At the back of the shop, behind the shopkeeper, were

small drawers with white china handles marked in blue writing with the names of the things inside, Flour, Sugar, Rice and Semolina. Johannes never tired of the shop, a place where you could buy whatever you wanted, whenever you wanted. No one ever needed a ration book to shop there. The old ladies never allowed Kathrin to play with the shop because, they said, she would swallow the tiny beads which were supposed to be rice or make a terrible mess of everything, so it was on a table where she couldn't reach it.

But when Kathrin tired of playing with the dolls and they had helped her to put them to rest in the pram and in the beautiful white, wrought-iron cradle where they rocked the baby dolls to sleep, Tante Clara, the oldest of the two sisters, would reach down an enormous box for her, and together they would set up the zoo.

Then, Johannes would leave his shop and sit down on the floor beside them and listen to Tante Clara's marvellous stories about the zoo and about the days when Berlin Zoo was first begun. They had never been to the zoo, but Tante Clara told them all about the animals, how big they were and what they liked to eat best. The noises she made to show Johannes what the animals sounded like were horrific. Johannes thought he'd be far too scared to go and see a real lion, but he liked to play with the wooden ones. Tante Clara's father had been a founder member of the Zoological Society, she said, and when she was a child they used to go to the Zoological Gardens every Sunday.

She shook her head sadly whenever she talked about what had become of the zoo nowadays. "You couldn't call it a Zoological Garden any longer," she said, "not like it used to be." They had no meat to feed the big cats any more, she said, and they would all have to be put down. And the animals were all neglected because there weren't enough zookeepers. Tante Clara would have been even sadder if she could have foreseen what would happen in November that year, when an air raid totally destroyed the zoo and all but a few of the animals were killed.

Now that their mother worked in the same factory as Evi, Kathrin and Johannes could wander up and down the stairs almost as much as they wanted during the day. But they weren't allowed to go outside, in case there were unexploded bombs in the ruins near their house. And they weren't allowed to go upstairs to Tante Clara and Tante Hilde in the afternoons because, their mother said, they were very old and needed their afternoon nap. So, after spending a morning with the shop or at the zoo, they had something to eat in their own flat with the old man and lady and the quiet, shy granddaughter who never left their side. And then Johannes would read to Kathrin, or they would ring someone else's bell and find some other children to keep them company.

They had a good time that year, 1943. Of course, there were still the air raids, and Johannes was still scared stiff when they had to run to an air raid shelter with the sirens wailing and droning on and on and on. But now, for the first time in his life, he had plenty of friends. Gradually, he had learned to relax and talk to all the older people in the house, and he discovered he wasn't frightened of the other children as he had been frightened of Wolf in Oberdorf.

Nobody seemed to mind either when all the children in the house made a terrible noise playing football in the long, long hallway which stretched from the front door right to the back of the house. Sometimes even the old man living in the flat opposite to Evi's would stand in his doorway urging them on, showing them how to kick properly, while Kathrin ran up and down, dodging round them, or spoiling everything by running away with the ball, squealing with laughter.

7

Their mother always worked on Saturdays, but one Sunday in August they even went for a day out to the suburb of Berlin where they had lived with Oma and Opa. "We can see if Tante Ursula is still there, or Onkel Rolf," their mother said. They hadn't heard from Tante Ursula or Onkel Rolf and his wife for a year or two. It was hard to keep in touch with people when whole streets had been destroyed.

When the postman had any letters for their street he used to walk round shouting, "Is anyone around here expecting a letter?" and then people had to show him their papers and tell him their name before he would give them the letter. So it was no surprise that they hadn't heard from Tante Ursula. Onkel Rolf was a doctor. He was far too busy to write letters anyway.

It took them a long time to get to Lichterfelde. For a start, it took them ages to get on a train because soldiers always had priority when the trains were crowded, and there were plenty of soldiers travelling towards Lichterfelde, where there was a huge officers' training camp.

When they got to the station at Lichterfelde West, there was a group of young soldiers in smart new uniforms waiting to board another train. One of them suddenly slapped Johannes on the back. It was Wolf. "We're off to France," he said, proudly. "I bet you wish you were coming, eh?" He waved his rifle and said, mockingly, "But you're still far too young and far too small."

Johannes' mother turned round and saw him too. "And you're far too young as well, Wolf," she said. "You may be a great giraffe of a lad, with your long legs, but I know how old you are and you're no more than fifteen." Wolf was angry. The other young soldiers were laughing at him. "That's where you're wrong," he said, going red in the face. "I'm sixteen now, and at sixteen I'm old enough to join the army." "God preserve us. You don't know what you're doing," said Johannes' mother. Wolf's company was summoned onto the train, and they marched smartly off, with much clicking of heels and clanking of rifles.

Johannes walked out of the station with his mother and Kathrin. His mother seemed to be in a hurry, but the first place she headed for was not Tante Ursula's but the army barracks. She had travelled all that way hoping to get news of her husband, and she was terribly disappointed when there was none.

Johannes couldn't understand the fuss she was making. He had stopped thinking of his father, except when their mother spoke of him and showed them his photo, and Kathrin had never even known him. Johannes assumed that one day they would hear that he was dead, like Onkel Christian, but he didn't think he would mind.

Only his mother seemed to mind. She didn't seem to notice how well they were managing, how much fun they were having in the house with all their friends. She was always saying things like, "You poor, poor children. One day your father will come back, and then everything will be much better." Johannes couldn't see how things could get better. He didn't feel he was missing anything.

Their mother was depressed and very irritable when they left the barracks. It was a hot, hot day and Kathrin's little legs trailed and dragged on the sandy streets. Her mother pulled on her arm and shook her. "Come along. Stop dragging your feet. There'll be no more shoes when you wear those ones out. I haven't got the money to keep buying you new things." When Kathrin still trailed her feet on the ground, she slapped her, leaving a red mark on her

49

legs, and Kathrin yelled all the way to Tante Ursula's.

The house was empty and all the shutters were closed. A lady who lived two houses down the road said she didn't know where they had gone. "I could swear they're all safe," she said. "I'm sure they all got safely to the shelter, in the last raid. I could swear I saw them there. But I don't know where they went afterwards. Perhaps they've got relatives in the country."

Johannes' mother nodded her head wearily. It was already getting too late to walk to Onkel Rolf's, and then, to make matters worse, the air raid sirens began, first moaning softly and then getting louder and louder. "Where's the nearest shelter?" Johannes' mother asked an old man. Very small he was, with white hair and bloodshot eyes. "You come with me lassie, and I'll show you," he said. "I'll carry the little one for you if you want."

Johannes thought the man looked so old that he could do with being carried himself, but he picked Kathrin up and walked off, urging them to follow him. "We can go to the cellar of our church," he said, "the church of the Holy Family. It's just round this corner, then a bit of a way, and see," he motioned with his head, "you can see the tower already. We just go round that corner down there, past that big house and we're there. No distance at all, and the cellar's rock solid. They could drop ten bombs right on the church itself, and you wouldn't feel a thing in the cellar."

"Thank you so much for helping us," said Johannes' mother, trotting along behind him and quite out of breath because the old man was walking so fast. "Oh, no problem," said the old man. "If there's one thing I love more than anything else, it's children—especially little beauties like this one," and he put Kathrin down at the gate of the churchyard. "Now, little ton-of-bricks, you can run the rest of the way by yourself. It's a beautiful church, you know," he went on, "but there's no time to show it you now. Mind you, it's not looking at its best at the moment. The problem is, we can't get glass to repair the windows from the last time it was damaged—in March. They say churches aren't important for the war effort so they won't give us any building materials."

Johannes wondered why they were bothered about mending the windows when they would probably just get blown out again in the next bombing raids.

It was a lovely summer evening, still bright sunshine at eight o'clock. It seemed such a pity to have to go down into the gloomy cellar, but the sirens were still wailing, and there were other people now, hurrying towards the church.

When they had been inside for a while, everything went quiet. The sirens stopped and all the people waited in the eerie silence for the first explosion. Then it came, a low rumbling noise rising to a crescendo and the cellar rocked like a ship on a stormy sea.

The electric light went out after the first bomb, and then Johannes lost count of how many other explosions there were till the all-clear signal was given. They all just sat in the dark, terrified, as what seemed like a great giant with a battering ram beat incessantly at the doors, on the walls and on the ceiling. Any moment now he would smash a huge hole through the roof, and they would all be dead. Johannes was frightened. He tried desperately to see in the dark, to see where the dreadful noises were coming from. But Kathrin, weary of trotting round all the hot, dusty day, was fast asleep.

When they emerged from the cellar, the whole of the sky to the east of the church was a sea of flames. They had gone into the cellar on a day of heavenly sunshine. When they came out, it was night and the sight which greeted them was more like Hell. For days afterwards a dirty brown cloud of smoke blocked out the sun all over Berlin.

51

From the church they set off walking for the station, refusing the old man's offer of hospitality and wishing him good luck. Johannes' mother insisted that she had to get home so she wouldn't be late for work the next morning. But it couldn't be helped. She would have to be late after all. There were no trains till eight o'clock in the morning. They sat on the station platform for five hours, sometimes dozing, and sometimes coughing because of the stinging smoke which was drifting around, stabbing at their eyes and throats. At least the trains were running.

"We're lucky that the trains are running, aren't we?" said Johannes, meaning to be helpful. His mother didn't pay any attention to him. Either she was asleep or ignoring him. He looked sideways at her, sitting on the bench with Kathrin cradled on her knee. Her eyes were open, so she wasn't asleep, but she was staring at the opposite side of the platform. She looked very, very sad. "When father comes home it will get better," he said to her, putting his hand onto hers. He didn't know what else he could say.

8

After that time in the church cellar, there had been a break in the big, serious bombing raids, and Johannes had been able to forget his fears and enjoy himself again, playing with the other children in the house, and with the zoo and the shop upstairs in Tante Clara's flat.

Of course they weren't real aunts and uncles, the old people in the house, but they meant more to Johannes than Tante Ursula and Onkel Rolf whom he couldn't ever remember having seen. "Your real relatives are the ones who'll help you when you need help," Johannes' mother used to say. "You can't just go to anyone when you need something. Relatives have a duty to help you."

But Johannes was far more sure he could get help from Tante Clara than from an uncle or an aunt he had never seen. Tante Clara lent him books now as well, books about animals and about Red Indians. She had a whole set of Karl May books, about life on the wild frontiers, but she would only let him borrow them one at a time. He read them sometimes in the afternoons when his mother was out at work, and then in the evenings when she was so tired and sad after work that she didn't even seem to want to talk to him.

Once a week, on Sundays, his mother made him sit down and write a letter to his father, which Johannes thought was very unfair as his father never wrote to them. He could never think of anything to say. Sundays became more and more of a torture to him. He used to pray in church, "Please God, please let mother forget that we have to write letters today." But she never did.

One Sunday, Johannes sat for half an hour, not knowing

what to write, while his mother sat opposite him chewing the end of her pencil. She would write three words, then rub one out, then write again. Her progress was almost as slow as his. He didn't see why she should torture herself as well as him with writing to someone who never wrote back.

"How do you know he's still there?" Johannes asked suddenly, defiantly. "Who's where?" she said impatiently, rubbing out something she had just written. "How do you know father's still at the place you always send the letters to—seeing as he never answers them?" "I'm sure they forward them. They always have done till now," snapped his mother. "Don't ask such stupid questions. I'm trying to think."

"How do you know he isn't dead, like Onkel Christian?" persisted Johannes. "It happens to most people who go out East. Evi told me." "Evi doesn't know a thing about it," answered his mother. "Your father hasn't even been wounded, or they would have told me. And certainly they would have let us know if he was dead. I don't know why Evi needs to put such stupid ideas into your head."

That night a whole series of air raids began, which continued night after night for more than two weeks. Every night was the same, stumbling out into the cold, making their way through the freezing fog and the smoke which was still heavy in the air from the bombings the night before. One night the bombs hit a part of the factory where Evi and Johannes' mother worked, not the part which was important for the production of weapons, but the part where huts had been quickly thrown up to house the homeless women workers and the foreign prisoners of war who worked there. All the other workers, including Johannes' mother, were expected to turn up the next morning as usual to help with clearing up, so that production of bombs would be interrupted as little as possible.

One night the zoo was demolished, killing all but ninety-one of the thousands of animals which had been kept there. That was the day all transport, public or otherwise, ground to a halt in Berlin, and everyone went everywhere on foot or by bike.

But Johannes was always amazed at how quickly things got back to normal after the air raids which were meant to break everyone's spirits. He knew that the enemy wanted to break their spirits, because Goebbels always said so on the radio. He always added that everyone must work even harder for the war effort, to show the enemy that German spirits could not be broken.

And it was true. The air raids, which were meant to force the Berliners to get their leaders to surrender, made people more determined than ever to fight the terrible British devils who were pouring death by fire out of the sky. People didn't complain all that much. Johannes' mother never complained about having to go to work after a harrowing night in the air raid shelter, which always carried on into the early morning when she would have to help fight fires or shovel heaps of rubble off the pavements to clear them for people hurrying to work.

It was amazing how life got back to normal. After a temporary hiccup in the electricity supply caused by some cable being hit, the lights would usually come on again and then the radio would start again, blasting out merry music, or the latest announcements about the need for people to tighten their belts.

The message from the radio seemed to be that if only people were content with less food to fill their aching stomachs and less fuel to heat their ice-cold flats, the war could be won in the twinkling of an eye. Everyone had to make sacrifices. No sacrifice was too great for the Fatherland. These messages, coming across loud and clear over the radio, were punctuated by bright, cheerful military march music, and, now and again, by announcements about the air raid situation—much like the radio announcements we have nowadays about the traffic on Bank Holidays.

All this was normal life for Johannes. He listened a lot to the radio when his mother was at work. And when there was a two-week break in the bombings, as there was until 17th December, things had a chance to become even more normal. There were impromptu shops set up at the entrances to cellars, where the shop lady, with pitifully few things to sell, would keep both her hands on her wares to make sure nobody removed anything without paying in both money and ration book tickets. There were grandiose signs with gold lettering, over cellar entrances, declaring them to be the Berlin premises of the Royal Bank of Prussia or some other bank, complete with soberly suited, bespectacled bank manager. And in the Berlin Philharmonic Hall there were even orchestral concerts, conducted by a young man named Herbert von Karajan. Trams began to work and telephones began to ring, and then the whole thing stopped again suddenly when the bombers came back.

Johannes went over the Christmas Eve celebrations again in his head, as he sat propped up against the wall of the air raid shelter, his head nodding because he was so tired. He wasn't sure whether he had been asleep or not. He thought over what had happened before his mother had kissed him at bedtime and insisted that there would be no bombs tonight, that the British soldiers would be at home with their families too, on Christmas Eve.

They had been to church, he and his mother and Kathrin, and the church was very cold and damp because the glass had long since been blown out of the windows and the roof leaked, making water collect in huge puddles on the uneven stone floors. The priest had prayed for all

56

the soldiers who had died or were wounded in the East, and then for all the people who had been made homeless by the bombings. And he appealed to them to take in anybody who didn't have anywhere to lay their head that night—just as the Holy Family had no place to stay in Bethlehem.

They were still very lucky, and Johannes knew that. Their house was still standing and the people in it were all healthy and happy and had all met in the enormous hall to wish each other a wonderful, peaceful Christmas, as if there was no war to disturb that peace. The adults had all saved from their ration books, and somehow they had managed to get hold of some gingerbread and even some dates for the children.

Before they went to sleep, Johannes' mother made them pray again, even though they had already done their praying in church. They prayed for father's safe return, and then they prayed that Germany would be protected from an invasion by the Russians. Johannes' mother told him terrible stories about what would happen to the women and children if the Germans lost the war and the Russians moved into Berlin.

Johannes didn't like to think about that, so they had to pray for victory. He asked his mother, "If I pray for us to win the war, and an English child prays for England to win, who does God listen to?" His mother answered slowly, "He listens to the side who are in the right."

And then the howling, sobbing air raid sirens had wrenched him out of his sleep. The British must be in the wrong if they dropped bombs on women and children, on houses and churches and zoos indiscriminately. So did that mean the German people were in the right? His mother usually said, "We've just got to put our trust in God, and he'll do what's right for us."

Suddenly Johannes was jerked out of his half-sleep and even Kathrin woke up and looked all around with her huge, sleepy, blue eyes, when an air raid warden came rushing into the shelter, shouting, "We need fire fighters. There are some houses partly on fire, where a fire bomb had landed on the roof and needs to be checked before the whole house goes up. We need all the help we can get."

Johannes' mother made Kathrin stand up and pushed her over to Johannes. "Look after Kathrin for a while," she said. "You two stay here and I'll see what I can do to help." She went outside with four or five others, and soon Johannes and Kathrin were feeling fresh earthquakes as more bombs fell on and around their shelter.

After what seemed like ages, one of the men who had gone out to help, the man with only one leg, came hopping back into the shelter. "You wouldn't believe it," he said, "just when we need water the most, it's always cut off at the mains. How do they expect us to fight fires when there's never enough water to do the job properly? It's a good thing some people have the foresight to keep their baths filled."

"Where's my mother?" Kathrin went up to the man and asked him as he sat slumped in a corner, wheezing and trying to get his breath back. "Oh, they went on to do another house," the man explained. "They said they didn't need more than four for that job, so I left 'em to it. Things don't get so hot down here." He shivered, and laughed at his own joke.

The man was still the only one who had come back into the shelter by the time the all-clear signal was given, and Johannes knew at once that something terrible must have happened to his mother. "Where's my mother now?" Kathrin asked the man again, and he said, "They must still be hard at work out there. I wouldn't worry if I were you. Run along home now. Out there's no place for a child. Rather them than me," he said to himself, as he picked up his rucksack and hopped out of the shelter.

9

Kathrin and Johannes sat there and waited a little longer, even though the shelter was empty. Then they went up the winding stairs to the entrance. "Where's our mother?" asked Kathrin. Johannes wished he could say, "She's probably gone to work. It's already morning"—although the thick brown smoke made it difficult to say what time of the day or night it was. But then he realised it was Christmas Day.

There was no factory to go to on Christmas Day. He remembered that Tante Clara had said they could go up to her flat with their mother on Christmas Day and see what little surprise she had for them. Johannes lied to Kathrin. He was no longer sure of anything, but he said, "I'm sure she's helping to clear up the mess somewhere. Perhaps a cellar has fallen in with some people inside. She must be digging somewhere. We'd better wait here for her, because if she can't come herself she'll send someone to tell us where she is."

They waited a long time, but no one came to the poor, cold children. Sometimes they sat on the step at the entrance to the shelter and sometimes they ran up and down the pavement to keep warm. Everywhere around them there were small fires burning in the ruins, but Johannes knew they musn't go near them in case there were unexploded bombs about.

He comforted Kathrin when she cried. No matter how warmly her feet were wrapped up she still seemed to get chilblains, and they hurt her now more than ever, sitting out in the cold for so long. It all seemed so quiet, after the noise and excitement of the night before. And there were no people about. Most of the people from their house used another shelter, not so far away from where they lived, but their mother had always said that it wasn't so safe because it had been built earlier in the war when the bombs weren't so powerful.

The area around the shelter they had come to had been badly hit in August, and almost nobody lived there any more. They were alone in a bleak forest of smouldering, black, charred wood, of strange broken bits of iron reaching like twisted, tortured arms up to the sky.

The sun never did manage to struggle through the dense sea of smoke which swallowed up the city, but when he thought it was about midday, Johannes carefully opened their suitcase and took out a piece of bread for each of them. There was more bread, but he knew how important it was not to eat everything at once. He shut the suitcase, and they sat down on the steps again, eating their bread, and looking and listening for any sound which might tell them that someone was coming, sent by their mother to look after them.

Johannes knew instinctively that his mother wouldn't come back any more. But he didn't want to tell Kathrin, not yet. By late afternoon, he got fed up with her questions, "Where's our mother? When's our mother coming? Why doesn't she tell the people she's helping that we're waiting for her? We've been waiting so long."

Johannes' sadness made him weary. It was a heavy load to carry, this certainty that his mother would never come back. But he had to look after Kathrin. His mother had always told him that was his job.

After they had waited a little longer and still no one came, he decided to go back to their house. They walked quickly along the few roads which separated the shelter from the house. In the second road, a soldier was standing by a charred wall which still had a pretty patterned wallpaper on it, all that remained of what had once been a large house with fifteen flats.

"Hallo, lad," he said to Johannes, "perhaps you can help me. Do you know when this house was bombed, or where all the people went to?" Johannes gazed round at the ruins of all the houses. Only one or two were still standing. His mind was blurred. He couldn't remember what it had all looked like before the last air raid. He couldn't even remember whether that house had still been there the day before, though they must have passed it, on their way to church and then on their way to the shelter.

The soldier thought Johannes was a bit simple because he just kept staring round him then gazing speechlessly at the soldier and then back at the house. Johannes really couldn't recall a time when the streets of Berlin had looked any different. He was hungry and his mind was a blank.

The soldier bent down to Kathrin, "Was this house still standing yesterday?" he asked, more urgently. "Oh, yes!" said Kathrin with a beaming smile. "And in the window they even had a Christmas tree. Mother said they'd get shouted at for showing a light. You're not supposed to show lights at night, you know," she added. "But when we were on our way to church, they even had their curtains open to show the tree. Mother said it probably didn't matter on Christmas Eve, that no bombers would come on Christmas Eve. But," here she shrugged her shoulders and held her little hands out in a gesture of resignation, "they just came."

Johannes' head ached. Kathrin was a chatterbox. There was no stopping her, once she started. "Thanks, little one," said the soldier, patting her blond curly head. "How old are you?" "Three," she answered proudly. "So big?" The soldier took something out of his pocket. "Here, my little girl's as old as you." He had given Kathrin some gingerbread.

He pointed to the pretty patterned wallpaper. "That was our living-room. When I went away, I thought I'd have to redecorate it when I came back, because it was already getting a bit tatty. But Hitler's saved me the trouble, hasn't he? Him and the British bombers." He lit a cigarette. Johannes saw that his hands were shaking and watched him in silence as he took a piece of chalk out of his pocket, and began to write on the wall.

"What does that say?" Kathrin asked the soldier. Johannes slowly read it out loud as the soldier wrote— "Liesl, I have gone back to barracks. I'll come and look for you here again tomorrow morning." The soldier paused and then wrote "Merry Christmas." "My wife'll see that when she comes back here. She's expecting me, you see," he explained to Kathrin. Johannes asked him, "Please may I have some chalk? Perhaps we'll need to leave a message for our mother one day." The soldier broke his piece in half. "Good luck, lad," he said, patted Kathrin's head again and went off.

Johannes and Kathrin walked on to where their house had been. From the other end of the road, they could hear a constant banging and drilling noise, but they couldn't see anything further than the next house because of the smoke which hung over everything. Only the walls of Evi's flat were still standing.

Kathrin burst out crying. "Now how shall we find mother?" she wailed, and then sat down on a piece of wall, sobbing. "She's nowhere round here. And there's nobody else either. Where's Tante Clara? She looks after us when Mami's not there. Where's Evi?" Johannes put his arm round her. "Don't worry, Kathrin. Don't worry. God will look after us." They were the first words which came into his head, the words his mother often used to comfort them—though he already had his doubts about God, about what happened to all the things they asked him for when

62

they said their prayers, things that never happened, no matter how much they prayed.

Johannes saw that the outside entrance door to their cellar was off its hinges, and he pushed his way inside. "Come on, Kathrin. Perhaps we can stay here—in case mother comes back to get us." He took his piece of chalk and wrote in big letters on the outside wall, near where the front door had been, "Mother, we're in the cellar." "You must write Merry Christmas," said Kathrin, "—like the soldier did." So he wrote that too. He was beginning to be hopeful. Perhaps their mother would come back. Perhaps she had been working all day with rescue workers and hadn't had time to come back to look for them.

They went carefully down the steps into the cellar. There was no light, but it wasn't too dark because there were three or four small slits of windows right up near the roof, and Johannes lit a candle as well, from their suitcase.

It was a very large cellar. Each flat had had its own private section, fenced off from the others, to keep wine or bottles of fruit, potatoes and furniture in store. But the bombs which hit the house must have shaken the cellar so violently that everything was broken open. The wicker gates to each separate part of the cellar, which were normally padlocked, were hanging off their hinges. Everywhere there was broken glass from wine and fruit bottles and there were dented tins and battered suitcases all thrown together by the force of the blast.

The children found one jar of plums which hadn't been broken so the first thing they did was to sit down and eat from that, drinking the sweet, sugary juice when the plums were all gone. And then there were lots of things to explore. In one sealed cardboard box, there were countless small boxes of sugar lumps, so they ate as many of those as they could, till they both felt rather sick. They hadn't had so many sweet things for years.

In one corner of the cellar which was relatively undisturbed they came across a doll's pram, pale green it was, shaped at the side like a sea shell, and with metal wheels and a wrought-iron handle. There were three beautiful dolls at the head end, and a very old bear at their feet. "I think that belongs to Tante Clara," said Kathrin. She pointed to where the upstairs should have been. "The one upstairs belongs to Tante Emma."

"I don't think they'll mind if you have it," said Johannes. "They wanted to give you something special for Christmas. Perhaps that was what they were thinking of." Johannes couldn't understand where everyone from the house had gone to. He knew that people usually came back to bombed-out houses, to salvage whatever they could from the wreckage. He, like Kathrin, wanted to cry out, "Where's Tante Clara? Where's Tante Evi?" But there was no one to ask.

Whenever Kathrin asked where they were, he told her to shut up and stop asking him stupid questions. At long last, she grew tired of asking questions and tired of playing with the beautiful dolls, so Johannes laid out his mother's extra cardigan from the suitcase and a blanket from the doll's pram for a pillow, on an old, dampish mattress. Kathrin grinned at him as she lay down, and said, "It was a good Christmas Day in the end, wasn't it?" She fell asleep almost immediately with one of the dolls in her arms.

Johannes couldn't fall asleep so quickly. He was already worrying about what the next night and day would bring. He first made sure their suitcase was ready with their papers and ration books, some food and extra warm clothes in case of an air raid warning—just as he knew his mother did every night. Then he went round the cellar, rooting in any old suitcases or boxes which weren't badly damaged.

The pram would make a good carriage for transporting

things. He decided one doll would have to be enough for Kathrin, so he pulled out the other two dolls and the bear and put them on the floor. He tucked the things he had found underneath the blankets—more sugar lumps, two packets of pumpernickel, a tin of sardines, a jar of apple purée. Then he put the old, battered bear back in on top of everything, on the pretty lacey pillowcase.

He realised that he had had his pyjamas on all day, underneath his overcoat, so he changed into his daytime clothes and stuffed the pyjamas into the suitcase. His mother had dressed Kathrin up in a pair of his old, warm trousers and a pullover on top of her night-dress, so he decided not to disturb her. He thought it was probably too cold to undress her down in the cellar anyway. He checked once more to see if they had everything ready in case of an air raid warning. And only then did he lie down to sleep, on the mattress, with his arm round Kathrin.

10

When they woke up the next morning, Johannes was surprised at first that there had been no air raid during the night. It was obviously quite late in the morning. They could hear a loud noise outside, like engines revving up, but it wasn't the noise of planes, so there was nothing to worry about. They breakfasted on the bread which was still left in the suitcase, their mother's share, and then Johannes told Kathrin he had decided they should go and look for Onkel Rolf.

"But mother will be back soon," said Kathrin. "No she won't," said Johannes harshly, and then, more gently, "don't worry. I'll write another message on the wall, so that if she comes she'll know where to find us."

As they emerged from the cellar, Johannes dragging the pram up the steps, they realised that the loud noise they had heard outside was that of a pneumatic drill. Some soldiers were drilling a hole in the wall of a house where the cellar entrance had caved in, trapping some people inside. The drilling had been going on all night, but the soldiers in their steel helmets stopped when they saw Kathrin and Johannes.

"Hey! You two! You must be mad!" one of them shouted, running over to the children. "Didn't anyone tell you to keep away from those houses? There's still two bombs over there, unexploded. We cleared everyone out of this area just after the raid. Now run along home. This is no place for a child." He looked accusingly at Johannes. "You're old enough to know you shouldn't play in the ruins," he said, "and you must be crazy, bringing your little sister along too."

Kathrin gave him a big smile. "But we weren't playing," she said, "We're looking for our mother. Do you know where our mother is?" Johannes shut her up. "She's silly!" he said to the soldier. "Our mother's at work and she knows that very well."

He started to push the pram on past the soldiers with one hand, the suitcase in his other hand, and Kathrin tripped along after him. "We're on our way home now," Johannes called back to the soldiers. Kathrin looked puzzled, but Johannes didn't give her any explanation until the soldiers were well out of earshot, though they were obviously too busy to pay much attention to two dirty children with a doll's pram. They hadn't even noticed the suitcase.

When they had started their drilling work once more, Johannes said, "We don't want strangers to be helping us. They might make us go and live with them if they know we can't find our mother and father, and then mother would never be able to find us if she came to look for us. She always says relations are the ones to go to when you need help, so we'll go and find Onkel Rolf. We don't want to end up with strangers taking us to live with them; they'd probably separate us, send me to one place and you somewhere else, and then we'd never see each other again."

Kathrin raised one further objection. "We must go back. You didn't write a message on the wall for Mami." "If she comes looking for us, she'll know we've gone to Onkel Rolf's," Johannes reassured her. He had never seen Onkel Rolf, and all he knew of him was that he was a doctor and lived with his family in Lichterfelde West.

They walked past people sweeping broken glass from the pavement. "Why do they bother clearing up every day," asked Kathrin, "when there's always going to be more bombs coming in the night?"

Johannes didn't know. He said, "They have to clear the

pavements because otherwise children would fall over and might hurt themselves on broken bricks or glass."

Johannes knew the way to the underground station, and there was some money in his mother's purse in the suitcase. But a sign outside the underground said there would be no trains running till the next day. "We can sleep tonight in the church," said Johannes. "Father Hansen always says there's a warm welcome there for anyone with nowhere to go."

They pushed the pram back through the streets, avoiding their own street where the soldiers were still working, till they got to the church. The roof of one aisle had caved in, in the Christmas Eve bombings, and the other aisle was as Johannes remembered it, still full of the furniture which people had managed to rescue when they were bombed out. "Why did they bother rescuing it?" he thought, as the young assistant priest came towards them down the aisle.

"What can I do for you, little ones? Have you got a message for me from your mother?" he asked. Johannes didn't hesitate for one second. He had already planned what he was going to say. "Yes, Father. She says is it all right if we two sleep here for the night? We got bombed out, and she's taking us to Onkel Rolf's tomorrow, but she's working on night-shift tonight, so she can't come."

He seemed to speak without taking a breath, and as if he had learned it all off by heart. If there was one thing Johannes desperately wanted to avoid, it was to be taken in by the nuns; he'd had enough of them last year when they had taught him First Communion.

"The heating isn't on," said Father Heinrichs. "Since our pipes burst it's all broken down. But you can come and warm yourselves near the altar. Sister Anne has got a wonderful wood fire burning in that oven, and I'm sure she'll give you some soup if you ask her nicely."

Johannes didn't object to nuns giving him soup; he merely objected to them telling him what to do and how to behave. His mother had shouted at him for loudly voicing his objections to Sister Rosa's catechism class, so he hadn't objected out loud any more.

"Come and get yourselves warm," said Sister Anne, and some others who had been near the stove moved to make way for the newcomers. There were already about thirty people in the church, and it wasn't even dark yet. "You poor, cold little sparrows," said Sister Anne, "do you want some soup?" They nodded, holding out their hands for the bowls, and tucking in as soon as they were given a spoon. Kathrin had already eaten enough to have burned her lips when Sister Anne intoned a grace for them. "For what we are about to receive may the Lord make us truly thankful. Amen." The children were too hungry to be apologetic or polite.

"I expect your mother will be wanting some soon, when she comes along," said the young, rosy-faced nun, beaming pity and benevolence. "When's our mother coming? Have you seen her?" asked Kathrin eagerly. Johannes interrupted, impatiently, wanting to shut her up. "She's not coming tonight. I told you. She's on night-shift," he explained to the nun. "Tomorrow, we're all going to Onkel Rolf's together."

"That's very nice!" beamed Sister Anne. "You can stay here and keep warm till she comes for you." "No, no!" Johannes protested. "We're to meet her at the underground. She'll be very annoyed if we're late." The soup was watery, with leeks and carrots in, and what seemed like bits of pancakes, but it filled them up, temporarily. They were tired, and Johannes at least was struggling to hide his sadness. They both were glad to go to sleep very early, on the church benches. It was only just after six o'clock when they fell asleep—too early even for Father

Hansen's evening prayers.

In the morning they were stiff from lying on the hard benches, but Sister Anne had warm milk and bread to cheer them up. "We could stay here till mother comes back," whispered Kathrin. "With the nuns, we get more food than mother gives us." Johannes was bitter and decisive, bundling things into their suitcase and into the doll's pram while he was talking. "For the last time, we're not staying here," he whispered.

He waited until they were outside the church. "And mother probably won't come back—so now you know." He pushed the pram on faster, in silence, forcing Kathrin to run because she couldn't keep up with him. She said nothing all the time they were running to the underground station and while they were sitting on the train—just kept giving him frightened looks, which he ignored. He tried not to look at her. He thought that if she started crying, he wouldn't be able to stop himself from crying too and he didn't want to lose control.

An old lady on the train asked Kathrin where they were off to, and as she just looked stupidly at Johannes he had to reply for her. "Lichterfelde." "Phew! I don't know what you want to go there for," said the old lady. "Nothing there. Razed to the ground, it is. That's because of the Telefunken factory in Lichterfelde Ost, and all the barracks round that area." "Ah, but we're not going to Lichterfelde Ost," said Johannes, "Lichterfelde West is where my uncle lives." "Very nice too," said the old lady, who had reached her stop in Steglitz. "Well, good luck!"

A lot of people said that, Johannes had noticed. Good luck. Everything seemed to be a matter of luck. It was just bad luck that his mother happened to have been blown up somewhere, while helping to fight the fires. Very bad luck. He banged with his fist on the suitcase, his only expression of the rage which had been building up inside him. Kathrin looked at him, startled, her sad eyes searching him for some sign of hope or comfort. He went and sat beside her and held her hand. He felt helpless.

When they got off the train at Lichterfelde West it was still quite early—no later than ten o'clock in the morning. Johannes dragged the pram up the steps to the exit of the underground and then went back to get the suitcase. "You're too small to carry it," he said to Kathrin, panting as he got to the top of the steps.

He balanced the suitcase on the edge of the pram and pushed it away from the station, past the dance palace on his left, where there were posters out for an afternoon tea dance that day. Johannes stopped and stared at the West Bazaar shopping centre, across the tramlines on the other side of the road. He couldn't remember ever having seen such big shops before, though he had already been there in August, with his mother.

The enormous tobacconist shop on the corner seemed to be actually full of cigars and pipes and other wondrous things for sale in mysterious boxes. He had grown so used to shops which were just a table at the entrance to the cellar of a bombed-out house. Here, there seemed to be no queues of people desperate to get the last ounce of butter on offer. Nobody was in a hurry. Elegantly dressed ladies, and soldiers in smart uniforms stopped and chatted and then moved on.

While Johannes stared at the shops, Kathrin pulled at his arm. "When are we going to Onkel Rolf's? I'm cold. When are we going? What are you looking at?" Johannes wasn't thinking, when he answered her. "I don't know where Onkel Rolf lives," he said impatiently. Kathrin burst out crying and sat down on a doorstep. "I want my Mami!" she sobbed over and over again, at first getting louder and louder, but then subsiding into quiet crying which shook her whole thin little body.

71

"Don't be stupid!" Johannes shouted. Then he yelled at her, trying to drown out her noise. "Get up. You can't just sit there. It's freezing. Get up," and he pulled at one of her arms. But Kathrin carried on crying, pitifully. "Where's my Mami? I want my Mami." So Johannes tried persuasion. "Come on, Kathrin. If you stop crying and come, you can have a sugar lump."

She still kept on crying, and a little group of people began to gather round. "Come on, lass," said a man with glasses which were so thick that they made his face look thin inside them. "It can't be that bad. If you've lost your Mami we'll soon find her. She can't be dead, you know, if you've only just lost her. She's probably just gone into one of those shops over there. Just tell us where you last saw her, and we'll soon find out where she is."

Kathrin sobbed louder and louder, and Johannes grew red with shame and with the worry that they'd find out, then he and Kathrin would be taken off to live in an orphanage, perhaps even separated. He'd heard about that happening. The nuns had one place where they kept girls, and one place where they kept boys. He and Kathrin wouldn't be able to stay together if strangers found out they had no father and no mother.

"That child shouldn't be sitting on that cold step," said a very well-dressed lady. "That's no place for a child to be. She'll catch cold and then pneumonia. Her mother ought to be ashamed, leaving a little poppet like that alone on a day like this. Some people don't deserve to have children."

Johannes' face was burning with anger. "She isn't alone. I'm here to look after her. She just wanted to take her dolls for a walk and just now, when I wanted to turn back and go home to Onkel Rolf's, she started kicking up a fuss." "But where's your mother?" asked the elegant lady. "She's at my uncle's, waiting for us," answered Johannes quickly. "Now, will you come?" He pulled at Kathrin's arm but

72

still she sat on the step, listening to the conversation of the people gathered round her, fascinated by all the fuss she had caused.

"Perhaps she's tired," said the man with the thick glasses. "A little doll like her can't walk very far, you know. Look, if you'll tell me where your uncle lives, I'll carry her for you." Johannes said, "Oh no, no, you don't need to bother. She's a good walker." The elegant lady interrupted him. "Do you know where your uncle lives? He doesn't look old enough to be in charge of a small child," she said to the others, and then said, "How old are you? Five? Six? Mmm?"

Johannes was small for his age, but he wasn't going to accept being labelled as that small. "I'm eight," he said, "and my uncle lives down there." He pointed straight down the road. "He's a doctor, and our mother will be annoyed if we don't get home soon. We're going now, aren't we Kathrin?" This time, he didn't try to drag her to her feet, just held out his hand for her to hold. She pulled herself up, and had started pushing the pram off down the road before Johannes had even had time to say, "Thank you for calming her down. She's just a bit awkward sometimes. All three-year-olds are like that, you know," he said, with all the accumulated wisdom of his eight years.

The lady and the man with spectacles watched them as they crossed the road together and then went very purposefully down the street, past the ironmongers. "But why have they got that suitcase with them, if they were just taking the dolls for a walk?" asked the woman. She shuddered, not so much because of the cold, which her fur coat kept out very nicely, but at the thought of Johannes' dirty, defiant face as he had stood between Kathrin and the crowd of people. "Their mother ought to be put away, letting them get so filthy, and letting them wander around in the cold all alone," she said.

All that day the children walked round and round the streets of Lichterfelde West. They were lined with trees and with enormous villas, all built in totally different styles, and all, by their very solidity, firmly denying that there was any such thing as a war in progress. Some were built like castles, some like Roman villas, some were ornamented with young girls' heads and flowers and some were like Tudor manor houses, half-timbered, with places for window boxes in the summer. There were a lot of houses with fir trees in their gardens, still brightened up for Christmas, with tinsel and wooden painted figures.

Johannes looked carefully at the name-plates on every gatepost—especially at those which announced that a doctor lived in the house. But it was hopeless. They kept going round in circles. The only sign they had to show them that they had already been along one of the cobbled streets and checked all the names in that road, was the occasional house which had been damaged or destroyed by a bomb. These were so few and far between that they were useful landmarks.

Johannes wondered where they had lived with his grandparents, but he couldn't remember. It seemed such a long time ago now, the time when he had been almost as young as Kathrin, and eating all the cherries when he was supposed to be stoning them. It was hopeless. They had got more and more lost and it was getting dark.

They hadn't stopped to eat all day, because Johannes had kept on insisting they would find Onkel Rolf very soon. He never could eat when he was anxious or excited; his stomach just tied itself in knots, and he couldn't face the thought of food. This meant he was less than sympathetic to Kathrin when she complained of hunger. He also appreciated better than she did the need to conserve the little food that they had, to eat it up very, very slowly.

"You've only just eaten your bread. What more do you want?" he had said on the several occasions she had cried and said she was hungry. "And anyway, we had a good breakfast this morning." He could hear himself talking just as his mother had talked to him, all the time they had lived off rations and in their last year in Oberdorf. He had learned very early on to talk like an adult, even though it would be a long time before he learned to see things from an adult point of view.

But now he was ready to give up. His stomach and his legs both felt like going on strike at the same time. He was hungry and tired, and Kathrin kept on starting to cry, only shutting up when he shouted at her. The houses all around them seemed so unfriendly, because they were locked outside in the cold while other children were inside beside a warm fire.

A white bird, a plump, white pigeon, waddled complacently along in front of them and slipped through the wrought-iron gate of the next house they came to. "Even the pigeons round here have got plenty to eat," thought Johannes, leaning his head wearily against the gate and peering through it at the house, set back from the road by a large garden.

The house looked like an enormous wedding cake, yellow, with white stucco ornaments round windows and doors, and ornate white plaster balconies, as though it was covered in white and yellow icing sugar. From the double front door, which was raised above the lower ground floor windows, there was a curved flight of stone steps with wrought-iron hand rails that reminded Johannes of liquorice, the curly wheels of liquorice his grandfather used to buy him.

Somehow drawn to that particular house, Johannes slowly opened the gate which creaked a little on its hinges, and they both slipped inside, into the garden, leaving the pram and the suitcase just by the entrance. It was dusk, and the tinsel on the Christmas tree glimmered in the half light of the garden. But something else sparkled. There were apples and nuts draped round with tinsel hanging among the branches.

The children were both suddenly even more hungry. Johannes reached down one of the apples and gave it to Kathrin. "Come on, have one," he urged, "they must be there to be eaten."

They were both standing there eating in the frozen garden when they heard a rather thin, hoarse voice, quite close to them, coming from one of the windows. "Aha. I see someone's eating us out of house and home, my dear." The children carried on eating, too tired and hungry to bother about what happened to them any longer, and then suddenly, the man with thick spectacles whom they had seen near the station came out of the house and down the steps.

"I've caught your two culprits, mother," he shouted back to someone inside the house. "Don't you want to come in and get warm?" he said gently. "We won't do you any harm, don't worry." The man went and fetched the suitcase, and then he carried the pram carefully up the steps. "Come on," he said to the children, who were still standing at the bottom of the steps in the cold snow. "Mother's waiting. We can give you something better to eat than a few apples."

11

Inside, the house was even more splendid than it was outside, with thick, brightly coloured Persian rugs on the floor and enormous gilt-framed mirrors on the walls of the room into which they were taken. They were left there alone with a tall, thin old lady who wore thick glasses like her son's. She had very white hair and big teeth. Kathrin was afraid of her when she smiled at them.

"Don't be afraid. I don't bite," she said. "Come closer, so I can have a look at you. What a pretty little doll," she said, patting Kathrin's blond curls. "Where did you get your chubby cheeks from?"

Her son came in, and she said to him, "This little one! Just look at her, with her apple cheeks! Looks almost good enough to eat, doesn't she? But the boy needs a bit of fattening up, I'd say. You haven't had a good square meal for months, have you, lad?" she said to Johannes, pinching at one of his arms. "But we'll change all that. We'll soon fatten you up, won't we?"

"We knew you were coming, you know," she carried on. "We've been expecting you ever since my son saw you near the station. He said he could tell straightaway that you had nowhere to go. Well, what have you got for the poor little foundlings?" she asked, as her son came into the room a second time.

"I thought you'd like some pancakes," said the man, who was about as old as Onkel Christian. "Most children like pancakes, don't they?" Johannes and Kathrin had nothing to say. They didn't need to say anything. They just tucked into the pancakes, and then afterwards the man, Herr von Kempner, brought them more apples and nuts and told them to help themselves.

"They're from our garden, so they should be good," he said, watching them eat ravenously.

That night, after another, fatter lady had given them a hot bath, the children slept together in clean, white, warm beds in an attic bedroom. Johannes wasn't capable of making any more decisions for them. He just thought, as he fell asleep, "If we can rest here, perhaps they can tell us tomorrow where Onkel Rolf is."

The next morning, by careful questioning, the von Kempners were able to find out who Onkel Rolf was—a children's doctor who had moved with his family out into the country to be doctor to a newly founded orphanage for Berlin children. "If you go to him, he'll just plonk you in the orphanage as well," warned Frau von Kempner. "He's got four children of his own, so he won't want two more, especially as he hardly knew your mother. He's your father's brother, isn't he?"

Johannes had no idea. He only knew that his mother had meant to go to Onkel Rolf for help even though she hadn't seen him for years. Frau von Kempner saw his dejected look and said, "I'll tell you what we'll do; we'll notify the police and the Red Cross that your mother is missing, and they'll do all they can to find her. We can give them this address to contact you and you can stay here till they find her."

"Now, what about your father? Do you know which battalion he's with? We can write and tell him where you are as well." She had her pen already in her hand, sitting at the great desk in the study, and was waiting for an answer. Johannes merely shrugged his shoulders. "Don't know." She was amazed. "Come along!" she said. "Every little boy of your age knows which battalion his father belongs to, what rank he has and so on. A big boy of seven like you. You must know that."

"I'm eight," said Johannes, "but I don't know much about my father. I haven't seen him for a long time, you see. And he doesn't write to us very often," he added after a long pause. "When did he last write to you?" asked Frau von Kempner, drumming with her pen on the table. "Oh, he never writes to me," said Johannes, "even though mother made me write every week as soon as I knew how to write."

"When did he last write to your mother?" she asked, exasperated by his slowness. "A long time ago," answered Johannes. "Before last Christmas." "God, that sounds bad!" gasped Frau von Kempner. "Before Daniela went away," added Johannes slowly.

"Who's Daniela?" asked Frau von Kempner, her eyes suddenly sparkling into life again behind her thick glasses. "Is she your elder sister?" "I'm the oldest in our family," Johannes said proudly. "Daniela's the lady who let us stay in her flat. And she let me read her books. And she always wore a gold star on her dress, because Kathrin liked it so much. And one morning she went away in a lorry kissing and hugging all her friends, but she didn't say goodbye." "Bad, bad, bad!" said Frau von Kempner, putting down her pen.

Then she gave up the idea of trying to get any useful information out of Johannes. "Shall we see if the hens have laid any eggs, Kathrin?" she said, and went out into the garden to where there was a chicken run, giving Kathrin a large basket to carry. "They'll have to lay extra well while you're here, won't they?" she said. "So we'll give them some extra good food."

They took the eggs into the house and left them in the kitchen with the other lady, Frau Schenk, who did the cooking and cleaning in the house. "Are you allowed to keep the eggs, all of them?" asked Johannes in amazement, remembering the way inspectors had come to the farm in

Oberdorf to check that the family there didn't have more than their normal rations. "I don't see why we shouldn't be allowed to," said Frau von Kempner. "We're the ones who feed the hens and look after them."

There were a lot of things Johannes didn't understand about Frau von Kempner's household. He recalled Daniela's small flat in the house near Wittenbergplatz, and the way, after the bombings, homeless families had been moved in, so that there was just about one room for each family. The Kempner house had at least nine rooms, not counting Frau Schenk's flat downstairs—and all for only two people. He soon realised that most of the neighbouring houses were equally big and equally empty, just as if there were no war and no homeless people.

And then one day, Johannes asked Frau von Kempner something which had been on his mind for a long time. "Why doesn't Herr von Kempner go and fight in the army? All the men of his age are soldiers." She wasn't at all surprised or offended by his question.

"Several very good reasons. You can choose the best one. Firstly, his eyes are so bad that he couldn't hit a hippopotamus at close range. But nowadays they're so desperate for soldiers they'll take anyone, no matter what his state of health, just so long as he can drag himself to the battlefield and prop himself up long enough to be shot."

"Oh, no, that's not right," said Johannes, who had listened to the radio a lot while his mother had been out at work. He quoted a slogan which he used to listen to every day. "The German fighting force is the healthiest and most capable in the world. No German soldier dies without a bitter struggle and without taking at least one enemy soldier with him."

"That's as may be," said Frau von Kempner, cynically. "The fact is, they would have taken him, bad eyes and all, if he hadn't been working for the government."

"Oh, then he's doing his bit as well," Johannes rushed to reassure her. "It always says on the radio we musn't despise men who aren't soldiers, if they've got other important things to do for the war effort. They also serve who only stamp your ration books," he quoted again. "Everyone has to do their bit for the war effort. The harder we all work here at home, to support our soldiers at the Front, the sooner the war will be over."

"They ought to have you on the radio," said Frau von Kempner, drily. "They've certainly taught you well, but you still haven't heard the third reason why my son isn't a soldier. He would never be a soldier, even if he were as strong as an ox, and unemployed—because we object to killing people. And . . ." She came over to the table where he had been carefully drawing and colouring a picture of a tank, with a smiling soldier next to it.

She was a tall woman and she towered over him, her voice full of bitterness and her eyes full of hate, "and we refuse to fight for a country which is sick, with a leader like Hitler whose principles are vile and hateful." Johannes was absolutely shocked and frightened. His mother had always said she wasn't very interested in politics and politicians. He'd heard her saying that often enough in the air raid shelters when someone tried to strike up a conversation with her about the state of the country. But his mother always told him the good things Hitler had done for Germany. And the radio was always full of reports of his hard work and self-sacrifice for the German people.

And now here was Frau von Kempner saying all these terrible things. She looked like a witch when she towered over him like that. She was evil. Anyone who could say those dreadful things about Hitler must be evil. He wanted to take Kathrin by the hand and run away. But Kathrin was in the kitchen, baking biscuits with Frau Schenk, innocent of what Frau von Kempner was really like.

12

There were other times like this, which disturbed Johannes even more. Like the times when Frau von Kempner's friends came round and they listened together to the BBC German Language Service—the enemy radio. Johannes knew it was forbidden to listen to the radio from enemy countries, but the von Kempners didn't seem to take any notice of what was forbidden. They never made any attempt to turn the volume down, even if there was a knock on the door and visitors came. And all their visitors wanted to listen to the BBC as well, especially to the news.

One evening they were even more indiscreet than usual. Kathrin was asleep but Johannes was sitting in a corner of the room, reading. All the adults listened intently to the BBC news, with its reports of further bombings on the centre of Berlin and on other big cities in Germany. Herr von Kempner switched the radio off.

"Good God!" said one of Herr von Kempner's friends, another young man with thick glasses and sandy hair like the stubble in a corn field. Johannes never got to know the names of the visitors. "When are people going to realise? When's somebody going to get rid of Hitler? He's brought nothing but evil and sadness to Germany."

"That's a lie!" Johannes' voice rang out across the room. All the adults looked surprised. They had hardly noticed him before as he sat in the gloomy corner, reading one of Herr von Kempner's Karl May books. "You're lying," repeated Johannes, blushing now that everyone was looking at him. "Mother says that Hitler has done a lot of good for everyone. She says he got work for all the people who didn't have work before."

"Oh, no one can deny that," said Frau von Kempner. "He even had your mother working, didn't he? Mmm? Making bombs she was," she explained to everyone else. "Oh yes, he found work for your mother, all right, got her slaving from morning till night and leaving you all alone, when he used to say a woman's place was with her children at home. And now he's killing off our men so fast that he can find plenty of work for the ones that are left."

"Hitler isn't killing them!" Johannes was shocked. "That's a lie! It's the enemy who are killing them, the Russians and the British." Nobody contradicted Johannes. The six adults in the room just looked at him and he stared back at them, like a frightened animal at bay. "And he does do good things!" he almost screamed at them, going even redder in the face.

"Tante Bertha says it was Hitler who gave her her new radio—a brand new one, it was." Having blurted that out, Johannes marched to the door, but Frau von Kempner's words stopped him in his tracks before he could open it. "And how many of her sons did she give Hitler, in return for her lovely new radio?" Johannes just about managed to say, "I'm going to bed. Goodnight," before he left the room. He didn't want them to see him crying, but once outside the door, and all the way up the stairs he wept bitterly, confused and frightened of what he thought they might do to him.

"Awful little Fascist!" said Frau von Kempner to her guests. "I wouldn't have him in the house for one moment longer if it weren't for his adorable little sister. At least she hasn't been spoiled by political propaganda yet. We must take care he doesn't start putting those ideas into her head. There's no hope for Germany if even the children are growing up with ideas like that. He thinks everything good in this world comes from Hitler. It's all that rubbish that's blasted out on their precious radios all the time. It's a good thing he has lost both his parents, if that's the way they were bringing him up."

"Don't be hard on him, mother," said Herr von Kempner. "It isn't his fault that his head is full of such ideas. It may be his parents, or the state, but at the age of eight you can hardly blame him for what other people have told him to believe."

"Well, I don't like him," maintained Frau von Kempner. "If it wasn't for his sister I'd throw him out on his ear, for saying things like that in my house." "Try to like him," urged her son. "He's got a good heart."

In his bedroom in the attic, Johannes was lying on his bed fully clothed, crying quietly so as not to wake Kathrin. And yet he wanted to wake her. He wanted to shake her awake, take their suitcase and the pram (which were full of apples, nuts, sweets and raisins which he had stolen by degrees when Frau Schenk was busy in the kitchen), and to leave the house for ever. He was so sure that it was full of evil, dangerous people.

But something stopped him. He found himself crying, for the first time for his mother, who had always seemed to know what to do. He remembered how she had calmed him down when he was scared of the air raids, how she had stroked his head and held tightly onto his hand. He was lonely, lonely and grief-stricken, and angry because his mother had left them when he needed her most, left him to face these terrible strangers alone when she knew how shy he was. He wanted to run away, but he couldn't because of Kathrin. He knew instinctively, without waking her up and asking her, that she would refuse to go with him if he wanted to leave. In the five months since the von Kempners had taken them in, she had not only grown attached to the von Kempners but also to Frau Schenk, whom she now addressed as Tante Schenk.

She spent nearly all day and every day in the kitchen

with Frau Schenk listening to her songs and stories, emptying and sorting through her cupboards and drawers, "helping" her to do her baking and to lick the mixing bowls clean. More than once, when he burst into the kitchen of an afternoon, after he had finished school, Frau Schenk would put her finger on her lips and shake her head at him to be quiet, because Kathrin was blissfully asleep on her knee.

This made Johannes realise, to his horror, that Kathrin was already beginning to forget their mother. She didn't ask about her any longer, didn't seem to notice that she was missing. As Johannes looked at Kathrin, fast asleep in the attic, he knew for certain that she wouldn't leave the von Kempners because she already treated them as if they were her own family. And he couldn't leave her. She was the only person he had.

He sometimes tried to tell Kathrin how evil, how dangerous the von Kempners were, because he still felt it was his duty to get her away from them, to protect her from them. He had no idea where they could go next, but he felt certain they shouldn't stay there, with people who said such terrible things about Hitler. She just never seemed to understand; she was too young to understand how serious their crimes were.

Sometimes Johannes' teacher at school told them that it was their duty to let him know if any of their schoolmates or their friends or relatives said anything damaging about Hitler or about the army or the Nazi party, but Johannes never did tell him what he heard when the von Kempners had visitors, because he was thoroughly scared of what Frau von Kempner would do to him if she found out.

To please her son, Frau von Kempner did her best to be nice to Johannes, while at the same time trying to persuade him to change his ideas about what was good for Germany. He usually tried to escape out into the garden when she started to go on at him about Hitler, because he could only answer her with the things he had learned at school.

He knew his teacher must be right in the things he said about the enemy and about it being every man's duty to fight, because his teacher had been a soldier—till he lost both his legs in France. He often came to school in his uniform, and with his medals on, when it was a special national day of celebration, like Hitler's birthday. Johannes could believe what his teacher said far more easily than he could believe a silly woman who listened to the enemy radio. So he did his best to avoid any contact with Frau von Kempner, apart from at mealtimes, or when he absolutely had to go to her to ask her for some new school-book.

She still persevered, trying valiantly to be nice to him. For his ninth birthday, on 21st July 1944, she suggested they should hold a party for him. He had never had a birthday party in his life. There had never been enough food around to go inviting other people to share it. But the von Kempners always seemed to have enough to eat. They had never even noticed the bits of food Johannes kept on taking and stowing away—just in case he could persuade Kathrin to escape with him one day.

Frau von Kempner told Johannes he could ask five friends to his party, but there were only two boys in his class at school whom he knew at all well because he walked home with them. All the others had known each other a long time and didn't care to make friends with a new boy who didn't know anything like as much as they did.

Johannes was usually completely alone at school, but he was used to that. Most of the others had only begun to take notice of him at all when Frau von Kempner bought him some glasses, because the teacher had pointed out that he couldn't see the blackboard even when he sat at the front of the class. Then the other boys began to call him Four Eyes.

Rolf and Gerhard were sometimes nice to him. They

sometimes talked to him on the way home from school. So they were the ones he invited to his party.

They often said what a peculiar woman Frau von Kempner was, and they thought she was even more peculiar when she stopped Johannes joining the Hitler Youth Movement. An officer had called at the house to ask about that, about why she didn't let him join and Johannes had heard her telling him a downright lie. She said she needed Johannes to help her in the house and garden, because she was too old to do the work herself. But she never told the man she already had Frau Schenk as a helper. Johannes was the only boy in his class who didn't have a uniform to wear on special occasions, and he resented Frau von Kempner even more because of that.

Both Rolf and Gerhard wore their Hitler Youth uniforms as often as they could, and were always boasting about their fathers who were in the army, but who didn't actually go out to fight at the Front, because they were too busy training officer cadets at home in Berlin.

They wore their uniforms to Johannes' party and said "Heil Hitler" with a smart click of their heels when they arrived, just as they had to do at school every day. Johannes was embarrassed. Frau von Kempner didn't reply to them, but made them welcome when they shook her hand and bowed very formally, as they had seen their fathers doing.

Even though they didn't think much of Frau von Kempner, they were very appreciative of the cakes Frau Schenk had baked, and the three boys sat at a table out on the back lawn, wolfing them down. Then, after all the plates were cleared, Rolf and Gerhard sat back in their chairs as if to ask what was going to happen next.

"Why don't you take your friends up to your room, Johannes, and show them your birthday presents?" suggested Frau von Kempner. "Isn't Kathrin having her nap?" he asked nervously, knowing how little impressed the other boys would be by his birthday presents. "Don't worry about that," said Frau von Kempner. "She's curled up fast asleep on my bed, like a little kitten." Johannes hated to hear that. He hated the way Kathrin was so familiar with the von Kempners. She even kissed them, and sat on Herr von Kempner's knee every night with her arms round his neck, while he cuddled her and called her his little doll.

Johannes slowly climbed the stairs to the attic with Rolf and Gerhard. He was right. They were not at all impressed by his birthday presents. Herr von Kempner had given him a children's picture dictionary. "It's got rather good pictures," he said, showing them the picture of the man's insides which was next to A for abdomen.

He pushed his glasses up onto his nose nervously, but they made no comment, and only looked round for the next present. Then he showed them the new *lederhosen* Frau von Kempner had given him, and the long scarf which Frau Schenk had made. "Phew! You won't need that in this weather," was Rolf's only comment. "Where do you keep your toys?" asked Gerhard impatiently.

"Herr von Kempner lets me play with his chess set," said Johannes, and as this produced no reaction he added, "I used to have a toy shop to play with, before we were bombed out, and a zoo."

Gerhard gave Rolf a bored look and then shrugged his shoulders. "Let's go out into the garden," he said. "You can be the Russians, Johannes, and we'll be German soldiers, trying to flush you out of the hiding place where you're holding women and children hostage."

Johannes could run, but as far as Rolf and Gerhard were concerned he was hopeless at shooting with the gun they had made him out of a twig. They kept on stopping the game to tell Johannes the right way to shoot or where to hide himself.

Then Rolf decided they should show him how to make a fire in the wilderness. This he absolutely refused, because he said they weren't in the wilderness and Frau von Kempner would be mad if they set her garden on fire. So they gave up that game.

Johannes finally hit on a way to impress them when he offered to show them his secret house, a perfect hollow inside a clump of trees and bushes quite near to where Frau von Kempner always sat to drink her tea and read her newspaper on a summer evening. She was sitting there now, at the table, with a book in front of her which she wasn't reading.

They waited till she had gone inside for a moment and then slipped quietly across the lawn and into the hollow before she came back with another book. Inside the hollow tree there was yet more food, which Johannes had stowed away in the last few weeks since the weather had got so hot. "What a fantastic hideaway!" Rolf said. Suddenly he found Johannes far more interesting. "We could even sleep here one night," he said, "or run away from home."

"Sh!" said Johannes, "That's exactly what I'm going to do!" He lowered his voice even more. "I don't like her, and I don't trust her," glancing towards Frau von Kempner. Rolf nodded his head gravely. "I understand," was all he said.

They each sat and munched away at an apple, but Frau von Kempner didn't seem to notice them no matter how much they crunched and whispered. The thicket was just the right distance away to protect them from discovery.

Suddenly, Herr von Kempner came into the garden, waving a newspaper and shouting, "Just look at this. Have you seen this?" He always brought the newspaper on his way home from work. "I know what it is," said his mother calmly, "I heard it on the radio this afternoon. I just don't understand how it could have failed."

"Listen to this headline—" and Herr von Kempner read from his newspaper, " 'Attempt on Adolf Hitler's life. Fate preserved our leader. Our leader was unhurt—he resumed his work immediately.' God, the whole business stinks," he said. "If they'd given me the bomb I would have made sure it hit him, even if I had been killed at the same time."

Johannes had never seen Herr von Kempner so annoyed and disturbed before. He was staring straight over in their direction. They could see every detail of his face, but he was unable to see them. There were tears in his eyes as he said wearily, "It's a bitter blow for us. A bomb in his hand, and Stauffenberg still managed to miss Hitler. And we were all praying for him to succeed. Everything depended on him."

He shook his head, as if waking out of a deep sleep. "I wouldn't have missed him. And we won't bungle it the next time," he said, ripping the newspaper up and crumpling bits of it in his hand.

Two weeks later, on a Sunday morning, Herr von Kempner was arrested—for high treason. It had been reported that Herr von Kempner stated that he wished Hitler dead, on the afternoon of 21st July 1944.

Frau von Kempner looked in horror at Johannes when the men came, but Johannes hadn't betrayed him. He had grown to like Herr von Kempner, who had taught him to play chess, and always lent Johannes his books and pens. He was interested in what interested the children, so it was impossible for them not to like him. Johannes couldn't have betrayed him, but he knew who had done.

When they had taken him away, Kathrin, in tears, asked Frau von Kempner, "Why couldn't we stop the nasty men taking him away?"

"Because they have weapons and we don't."

13

Frau von Kempner hardly talked to Johannes in the next four weeks, but one morning she waved an official letter at him, which had come before breakfast. She had disappeared as soon as the letter arrived and only emerged a few hours later, her eyes red with crying. She found Johannes in the kitchen, where he was sitting with Kathrin and Frau Schenk and dragged him into the room which had been Herr von Kempner's study.

"You can read, can't you?" she said savagely. "Then read that, and see if you still think so highly of your friend Hitler." She sat down suddenly in an armchair, covering her face with her hands, while Johannes stood at the desk, reading.

In the first part of the letter, it said that Herr von Kempner had been sentenced to death for saying he wished Hitler were dead, and that the sentence had been carried out. The second part of the letter was a bill—the expenses of the execution, which Frau von Kempner was ordered to pay, so much for the hangman, so much for the prison officers, and so much for the coffin. And finally it was made clear that she was forbidden to put a notice in the newspapers about his death.

Frau von Kempner stood up, towering over Johannes, as he slowly finished the letter. Her red eyes and her blotched, bony face made her look like a witch, her eyes glittering with anger behind the thick glasses. "Now what do you think of your wonderful Hitler?" she almost spat at him. "Now can you stand there and say that he's done nothing but good for our country?"

Johannes was in despair. "But it wasn't him," he said,

"he didn't sign the letter. Look, it was signed by a man called Dr Haas. Hitler mustn't have known about it. He would have shown mercy on Herr von Kempner if he'd known."

After that Frau von Kempner didn't try to be friendly to Johannes any longer. She was cool and business-like in any dealings with him. Only with Kathrin was she still full of warmth and love, for the sake of her son, who had wanted to adopt the little girl.

"Things aren't going to get any better," she said briskly, one day in winter to Johannes, "so we'd better start teaching you what to do in case of emergency. You may as well make yourself useful. We haven't had many bombs around here, but that'll start one day too. Things aren't going to get any better," she repeated. "Now, what have they taught you in school about what to do in a bombing raid?"

She seemed to have forgotten the number of bombing raids Johannes had lived through already and he didn't remind her. Instead, he automatically ran through the list he had learned at school: a) always be prepared, with a suitcase or rucksack packed with papers, ration books, warm clothes and food; b) when the siren sounds, make straight for the nearest air raid shelter; c) have drinking water ready, and a damp handkerchief to put over the mouth because of danger of suffocation by smoke.

"And what do we keep in the cellar?" asked Frau von Kempner. "First Aid things, candles, matches." Johannes knew the list off by heart. "Oh, and we need sand, and we have to fill baths, sinks, everything possible with water to fight fires, in case the water gets turned off after an air raid. And we have to be ready to go out and fight fires if the air raid warden tells us to." "And as our nearest air raid shelter is our cellar, that's about all you need to know," said Frau von Kempner.

92

She had said things weren't going to get any better, and things were certainly getting worse by the day at school. One day they had a history lesson when the teacher had started to tell them how Jews were responsible for all wars, throughout history, even the war which was going on at the moment. Johannes didn't know about that. He'd heard people say it plenty of times before, on the radio, and in the air raid shelters, so he supposed it must be true.

But then the teacher began saying things which he knew just weren't true at all. The teacher was a thin, nervous man with a spotty, red face. He always became angry and excited whenever he began to talk about the war or about Jews. "The Jews wanted to have control over everything," he said, "control over the world banks, control over governments." His voice became more and more fierce and high-pitched as he spoke. "And they aren't fit to have control over the shops that most of them used to run in this country, robbing honest German people. Most Jews can't even read properly."

Johannes raised his hand, but his teacher, in full, eloquent flight, didn't want to be interrupted. "Questions afterwards. The Jews can count all right. They can count their money all right." A loud laugh came from most of the boys, and the teacher allowed himself the flicker of a smile at his own joke. "But you try teaching a Jew to read, as I used to do before the war. Impossible. All they were interested in was the mumbo-jumbo in their prayer books. And these were the people who wanted to take control over Germany. Hitler stepped in at just the right time. What date did the National Socialist Party come to power in Germany? You, Herbert, you haven't got your hand up—you tell me." But Herbert couldn't, and dutifully came out to the teacher to be thrashed.

Then, when some more eager boy had delivered the answer, the teacher turned to Johannes. "You, boy with the glasses, you had a question." Johannes went red in the face, because he didn't usually speak in class. He stood up, while they all looked at him. "Please, sir. I think you're wrong about Jews not being able to read. Our friend Daniela is a Jew, and she taught me how to read. And she didn't read religious books, sir. She had lots and lots of different ones, sir, because she used to work in a library. And she gave me some of her books, sir."

There was a silence which made Johannes look quickly all round in fright, as if some terrible monster had suddenly come into the classroom behind him. "Have you still got these books?" the teacher asked, coldly. "Because if so, you can bring them to school and we can burn them in the playground, along with anything else that your Jewish cow gave you."

"Have you still got them?" he repeated, staring keenly at Johannes. "No, sir. They were destroyed when we were bombed out." Johannes was lying. His mother had always put two books in the suitcase which they took with them to the air raid shelter, and Johannes still had two of Daniela's precious books tucked under the blankets in the doll's pram—one called *The Miraculous Car* by a man called Hans Striem, and his old favourite, *Hänsel and Gretel*. He had read both books over and over again, and he felt he would rather be punished himself than let them do anything to Daniela's books.

Johannes was taken outside by two of the bigger boys, and they thrashed him for contradicting the teacher, and for being friendly to Jews, and none of the other boys dared to speak to him any longer except to shout after him in the street, "Jew's friend! Parasite. Four-eyed friend of a Jew." Sometimes they followed him home in groups chanting and making animal noises, and threatening to beat him up, but usually they just ignored him.

His marks at school had been excellent until that day.

The teacher had been kind to him because of his father being a soldier in Russia; he had told the other boys that Johannes' father had died for the people, and they too had even been quite nice to Johannes for a few days.

But now that was all changed. Johannes' books arrived back covered in corrections. The teacher took every opportunity to tell him how stupid he was and ridiculed him when he read aloud, so that Johannes began to stammer when he had to read. The other boys had plenty of opportunity to mock him. Life was far worse than it had been before, worse even than when they had had to sleep in the air raid shelters every night with bombs dropping everywhere. Johannes had to go to school, but he was petrified and sick at the thought of going there every day, and at nights he couldn't sleep, because of what he knew it would be like in the morning.

One night, in his pyjamas, he wandered into Herr von Kempner's study, thinking he could read instead of sleeping. It was past midnight, but Frau von Kempner was sitting there in her son's armchair. "What do you want? What are you doing?" she asked, wanting him to get out of her way and go back to bed. He didn't answer, just stood there in the doorway, miserable and very small for his age, silhouetted against the hall light.

Frau von Kempner looked at him for a long time, and finally Johannes broke the silence between them. He wanted to cry, but he fought back the tears and said, his voice echoing in the silent, sleeping house, "Why don't you send me away, since you hate me so much?"

Frau von Kempner wanted to reply immediately, "Because of Kathrin. I love little Kathrin." But she looked at Johannes instead, looked at him for a long time. He was a skinny, unhappy young boy. He had never got any fatter, no matter how hard Frau Schenk had tried to feed him up. He stood blinking at her now, as his eyes got used to the dark, still peering at her in his pathetic, short-sighted way because he had left his glasses upstairs.

His mother and father were dead, of that she was convinced. And at the age of seven or eight he had taken on sole responsibility for protecting his sister—a responsibility which he still jealously guarded.

Frau von Kempner knew that Kathrin was sure of a loving and capable guardian in Johannes, for as long as she needed one. But at that moment it struck her how there was no one to love and protect him. In those few minutes as she looked at him and he stared back at her, shivering because he was standing on the stone floor of the hall and it was January, she realised too that she had been so busy repudiating the opinions of the influential adults who had found their way into Johannes' head that she had failed to notice what a child he still was. And suddenly she was able to see him as her son had seen him.

She went quickly to Johannes and knelt down beside him and pulled him towards her. "I don't hate you, Johannes," she said. "You've got a good, kind heart." Then she wrapped him in a tartan blanket which she sometimes had round her knees on a winter's evening, and, having bundled him up so that he couldn't walk, she carried him and sat him in her son's chair near the tiled oven in the wall.

She drew up a chair near to him, and then waited for him to tell her what was the matter. Johannes told her all about what had happened at school, with the teacher and the other boys. And Frau von Kempner only interrupted to say, "That was well done!" when Johannes came to the worst part of his crime, stopping the teacher and telling him he was wrong.

"Well, there's not really much I can do to help you," she said, when he had finished telling her about the misery and the mockery of the last few weeks. "You still have to go to school, so it's best if you don't run away from the problem. They're cowards and bullies, including the teacher, but we can't change them all of a sudden. The only thing you can do is to give them a good example by standing up for what you believe is right. I'm proud of you." She had said she couldn't help him, but she did help, simply by supporting the stand he had taken, when everyone else rejected and condemned him.

14

The war had still done comparatively little damage to the houses in Lichterfelde, though most people had lost someone from their family in the fighting. Since Herr von Kempner's death, food had become much more scarce in the von Kempner household. They now received much smaller rations, because they were no longer connected to someone who worked for the government.

Everyone in Berlin knew, in spite of the radio broadcasts to the contrary, that the enemy armies were getting closer, that Berlin would fall to the enemy in the near future. As Frau von Kempner and Johannes listened regularly to the BBC German Service, they were even more convinced that Berlin and the whole of Germany would soon be defeated.

Frau Schenk would sit in her kitchen with Kathrin, telling her what was going to happen, how the Russians were going to cut them to bits, so they'd better hide in the cellar, and how the Russians had threatened to starve them out of their homes or smoke them out.

Frau von Kempner was less extreme, but she too kept on telling them it would be far better to be taken prisoner by the Americans or the British than by the Russians. She too had heard too many reports about what the Russian soldiers did if they took women and children prisoner.

One day, after an air raid, she took Johannes and Kathrin to one corner of the cellar before they left it to go upstairs again. "Look, I've got something to show you, if ever anything happens." It was a small brown leather bag, and inside it were beautiful small pieces of jewellery, delicate chains with pendants, a gold charm bracelet, a pearl necklace, brooches and earrings. Johannes let them trickle through his hands, looking at each one and marvelling at them.

His mother had had a gold cross on a chain, and her wedding ring, but he'd never seen Frau von Kempner wearing any jewellery at all. "If ever anything happens," she said, "you must take this jewellery—for you and Kathrin. It may help you." Then she took the bag from Johannes, snapped it shut and put it back in the corner, beside some heavy gold clocks and gold-framed pictures she had brought down to the cellar for safe-keeping when the air raids began to get closer.

By the middle of April 1945, Berlin was surrounded by the enemy and they could hear the artillery fire getting closer and closer. Even so, Goebbels, on the radio and through the newspapers, was still urging everyone to fight back, still telling them it was possible for Germany to win the war if everyone, women and children included, played their part in the fighting.

Frau von Kempner thought it was a better idea for them to stay in the cellar if there was any fighting going on. They had a certain amount of food and water, and Johannes had taken care that there was sand as well, for fire fighting, but living in that part of Berlin he had almost forgotten the hellish fires and the phosphorous smoke, smouldering in the ruins for days after a bomb attack.

In Lichterfelde West, bombs had seemed to be accidental, like the terrible accident which had destroyed his grandparents' house. He had finally found the house, the ruins already picturesque with weeds growing over them, and it was the only house which had been affected in the whole of their very long street. Instead of the terrible desert of ruins he remembered near Daniela's house, there were empty spaces here and there in the rows of houses, like the gaps left when a tooth has fallen out. Or a house had had its roof blown off, or perhaps just a chimney.

At the end of April, a new sound shattered the sunshine and the springtime peace of the area where Johannes and Kathrin lived in Lichterfelde. It wasn't the alternately shrill and low moaning sound of the air raid sirens. It was the thunder of artillery fire, which couldn't be all that far away, since it shook the houses and made them rock at every explosion.

One day, while Kathrin and Frau Schenk were shopping at the West Bazaar near the station, a shell fell on the roof of a house just across the road from them, destroying the whole top floor, and crashing the Tyrolean wooden balcony onto the pavement below. But life was supposed to carry on as normal.

There was no electricity, and such a shortage of food that people were ordered to eat frogs and snails, young clover leaves and rape seeds, all things which weren't so easy to get hold of in the city when you either had a fairly small garden or no garden at all. Bakers had to be warned not to eke out their meagre supply of bread flour by adding sawdust or tree bark, so that must have been normal too.

But people can get used to all sorts of normality. In some suburbs of Berlin, Hitler's birthday was still celebrated on 20th April, just as it always had been since he had become the Führer.

But Frau Schenk couldn't keep up the pretence of normal life any longer. After much useless effort spent trying to persuade Frau von Kempner to let her at least take Kathrin with her, Frau Schenk moved, with her suitcase, to take up permanent residence in the cellars of the church of the Holy Family. She wasn't the only one. Long after the war was over, the parish priest admitted to sheltering twenty-five women and young girls in his presbytery at that time—all of them as frightened as Frau Schenk was about what the Russians would do to them if they found them.

On 1st May Johannes and Kathrin were both out in the garden, oblivious to the artillery fire, because even that was becoming normal. Kathrin, who was already missing Frau Schenk, was nagging at Johannes to read her a story, make her a daisy chain, fasten her doll's clothes, draw her a picture and perform all the other little tasks which Frau Schenk had always done for her. Johannes was trying to read, but she wouldn't leave him in peace.

Over to the west, there were traces of grey smoke in the air, but where they were the sky was a wonderful clear blue, with cherry blossoms silhouetted against it, throwing a reflection of their pale pink onto Kathrin's pleading face. Her white-blond curly hair gleamed in the sunshine and she laughed at him and then tickled him. "Come on, Hannes! Read me a story! I can't read!"

And then Frau von Kempner came out into the garden. "Bring your books down into the cellar if you want to read," she said briskly. "I don't think it's going to be safe to stay outside much longer. Can't you hear how close the firing is getting?" Johannes could hear, but he didn't want to go into the cellar. How wasteful to have to go inside on a day like this.

Kathrin went down the steps to the cellar only when Frau von Kempner offered to read her a story. Johannes followed reluctantly. They waited a long time, before the house began to shake violently with the force of shells exploding all around. Their cellar would have afforded little protection if a bomb had fallen directly on the house, but they didn't know that.

After one particularly violent explosion, followed by yet another dead silence, Frau von Kempner was convinced that a shell had actually fallen on one side of the house. "Come on," she said to Johannes. "Now you've got to put everything you've learned about fire fighting into operation. Come along. If there's a fire, we've got to get it put out before it engulfs the whole house."

Kathrin started screaming and sobbing hysterically. "No! Hannes, no! Don't leave me all alone. I'm frightened. I want to come with you both. Don't go, Hannes." "Silly goose of a girl," said Frau von Kempner. "Johannes can stay here while I go and have a look at what's happened. I can probably cope with it myself."

She went out at the garden entrance to the cellar, where Johannes was to hand her the fire buckets when she needed them.

With the first two buckets of water, she climbed out into the garden and then blinked in the bright sunshine and shouted back to Johannes, "I can't see a thing round here. I'll just look round the other side of the house." In the two minutes she was gone, Johannes heard the whistle and the dull thud which are the signs that a shell has landed. He turned round to Kathrin with his back to the door and then, a split second later, the explosion came, throwing him right back against the far wall of the cellar, where he lay on his face with cuts and bruises and a sprained elbow from the awkward way he had landed.

His glasses were broken, and the smoke in the cellar made it impossible for him to see anything anyway. But Kathrin was still alive. She was crying very, very quietly, still crying when she came over and touched him. "You aren't dead, Hannes?" He shook his aching head. "Blood," she said, and putting her hand up to his eyebrow she touched it and then showed him how much blood was on her hand.

He realised that the blood was running down his nose. It was hot when he tasted it. Kathrin held his hand, and Johannes sat in a daze, waiting for Frau von Kempner to come back and take care of him. Everything buzzed in his ears and in front of his eyes and he must have fainted for a short time. When he came to, Kathrin was standing in front of him. She had soaked the white lacy doll's pillow with water and was holding it pressed to his eyebrow. It was slowly turning red and pink, but the cold water made Johannes feel better.

He tried to push himself onto his feet, using his left arm, but the pain in his elbow was excruciating and he realised that he couldn't open his hand or turn it round palm upwards. There was only one position he could hold his arm in where it didn't hurt him.

He tried again to struggle to his feet, this time using his right arm to push himself off. Once he was standing up he felt suddenly sick and shaky again, as though he were going to keel right over. But he leaned for a few moments against the wall, panting and sweating from the shock and exertion.

He had dropped the doll's pillowcase. His eyebrow was bleeding heavily again and Kathrin gave him one of the handkerchiefs they always kept in the cellar to cover their faces if the smoke became unbearable after a bomb attack. "Can you put some water on it, please?" he had to ask her, surprised at how feeble his voice sounded, how sick and shaken he felt. But he decided that he wasn't hurt, at least not badly.

Because it was quiet outside they climbed up the cellar steps. The door had been blown off its hinges by the blast which had thrown Johannes to the back of the cellar. In the garden, where the cherry blossoms still waved their branches, undisturbed by anything but the wind, they found Frau Kempner's body.

Johannes lost all control. He screamed and screamed. Like a two-year-old child in a tantrum, he flung himself on the ground and screamed, "I want my mother. Where's my mother?" Kathrin stood silently beside him as he cried out over and over and over again, "Where's my mother?"

She was still standing over him protectively an hour later

when two Russian soldiers walked through the gate, with machine guns ready to fire. "What's the matter with him?" one of them asked. They couldn't speak German. "He's cut his head," suggested the other one, taking a good look at Johannes. The first soldier had walked carefully round the house and inspected the cellar entrance, his machine gun at the ready, and he came back to where Johannes was still crying.

"No use trying to calm him down for the moment," he said. "If you take a look over there you'll see why he's yelling. There's bits of his mother all over the place, and he keeps on saying something about *mutter*. That's the word for mother. Even I know that much German."

They wanted to carry Johannes away to their ambulance post, but Kathrin at first refused to go. She ran back into the cellar and managed to stuff the brown leather bag into the doll's pram before the soldier saw what she was doing, and then she imperiously ordered him, by the use of signs, to carry the pram up the cellar steps.

They walked slowly to the First Aid post near the station, Johannes, a thin, limp bundle in the first soldier's arms and Kathrin following on, proudly pushing her pram, just as she had always done when she went shopping with Frau Schenk.

15

On the next day, 2nd May 1945, the war in Germany was over. Johannes wasn't badly hurt. He had eight stitches where his left eyebrow had been and he hadn't been able to sleep on the mattress they had given him on the floor, because there was only one position he could lie in without his left elbow making him cry out with pain. Kathrin slept soundly beside him.

They were given a bowl of porridge in the morning and then the doctor said they could go. "You've got somewhere to go to, haven't you?" he asked. "Then run along home." The doctor was tired. He had worked through the night, looking after injured civilians and soldiers who had been brought in, and more were coming in all the time.

He assumed Johannes' mother had brought them in the night before, and now the beds were needed for people who were really badly injured. "You can wait outside till your mother comes. That arm will be all right," he said, as Johannes stood, hesitating. "Your stitches will need taking out in a week. You can come back here for that—that is, if we're still here." He was the only one who spoke German.

Johannes and Kathrin made their way out of the big dance palace on the corner near the station, past people who were lying wounded on the floor in the hall, on the landing, everywhere. A soldier helped Kathrin to carry her pram downstairs. "Better run along home now, youngsters," said the soldier in Russian, as he put the doll's pram down outside the door. "It's still not safe to be out on the streets."

As soon as he had gone, Johannes and Kathrin sat down again on the steps at the entrance to the dance palace.

Johannes had been thinking during the night, while he couldn't sleep. Frau von Kempner had told them it was best not to stay in Berlin, and they had no one there anyway.

Johannes had always been frightened of being sent to an orphanage before, of being separated from Kathrin. He was now even more scared of what the Russians would do if they found out that he and Kathrin had no father and mother. At first he thought they would be taken prisoner and sent to Russia. And then he thought again that perhaps it would be all right if they could find some relatives who would take them in and look after them.

Johannes only knew where two sets of relatives were to be found now, that is, if they hadn't been killed, which was also highly likely. First there were the people in Oberdorf, and Johannes was sure they wouldn't want to have two extra mouths to feed. And then there was Onkel Otto and Tante Edith and their cousins in Stuttgart. Johannes decided they would go to Stuttgart.

"The first thing we must do," he said to Kathrin, "is to go back to Frau von Kempner's house and get the brown leather bag she showed us, if it's still there." Kathrin beamed at him, then lifted up the base of the doll's pram to show him where she had hidden the bag.

The station was just across the road from where they were sitting. Nothing could be easier than to get on a train and go to Stuttgart. But there were no trains. After they had waited a whole day on the station platform, a soldier came up to them. "Move along youngsters. Haven't you got a home to go to?" They didn't understand him, so he brought along an officer who could speak some German. Johannes told him they had to go to their Onkel Otto in Stuttgart, that their Onkel Otto was expecting them.

The officer wanted to say they were a bit young for travelling all that way on their own, but he was getting used to the sight of children on their own, dragging suitcases, always in a hurry and always with somewhere they must get to urgently. It wasn't his business to look after all the stray children floating around at the end of the war. He had other things to do, like getting his men to mend the debris-strewn railway tracks so that the trains could begin moving again.

Johannes saw the officer hesitating. "We can pay for our journey," he said, and carefully removing the brown leather bag from the pram, he drew out the gold charm bracelet. The officer put the bracelet back in the bag, and the bag back in the pram. "I wouldn't go waving all that stuff around if I were you," he said. "If you have to use it, take out one thing at a time, in secret."

Then he began to talk in Russian again to the other soldier, so that Johannes and Kathrin had no idea what was going on. "Please take us to Stuttgart, please," said Kathrin. "I'll tell you what we can do," said the soldier finally. "Tomorrow there'll be a couple of ambulances going down south. You won't take up much room. We can shove you in one of those. It won't go all the way to Stuttgart, mind. You'll have to make your own way after that. Now run along home, and come back here tomorrow."

Johannes and Kathrin didn't move. "Go on! Get a move on" said one of the soldiers in Russian. The children could grasp what he meant, and they looked frightened, but still they didn't move. The officer shrugged his shoulders. "Well, if you're going to sleep here, you'd better sleep on a bench in there," and he took them to the ladies' waiting room. It had no roof, but still had three or four plush-covered benches.

Later on the officer came in with a square tin which had beans in it, and stood looking at them as they wolfed them down, shaking his head.

16

The next morning, a fleet of white ambulances arrived outside the dance palace. They were to take the Russian soldiers who could be moved to a better equipped base hospital further south, away from Berlin. The children had to sit on the floor between two stretcher cases, men who had lost their legs.

They slept most of the way, and couldn't speak German even when they did wake up, but Kathrin at least was happy with their transport. She had never ridden in a car before. "It feels as though we're flying," shouted Kathrin above the noise, as the ambulance bumped and rattled along the pot-holed motorways towards the south, "flying in a great, white, clumsy bird."

Johannes remembered his teacher telling him how the motorways were another thing they had Hitler to thank for. But Frau von Kempner had told him differently, told him how Hitler had only had the motorways built so that his soldiers and tanks could be transported quickly and efficiently to where they were needed in the fighting.

He couldn't feel as exuberant as Kathrin anyway. His left arm still hurt him so much that he thought he would never be able to use it again, and he still couldn't straighten it or turn the palm of his hand face upwards. It was totally stuck in one position, and when he tried to use it at all, he felt intense pain. His head throbbed and ached as well.

Twice, on the long, long journey down south he was sick, and Kathrin had to ask the soldier who was sitting next to the driver to stop the ambulance. He usually felt better after he had been sick, until it gradually got worse again.

Unable to eat anything when they stopped, there was nothing he could do except think about what it must feel like to have no legs. His teacher had had no legs, had always had a blanket covering the place where his legs should have been. But he had never shown that he was in pain, as these men obviously were, these Russian soldiers still in their uniforms. And all the invalids who were bring driven down south were supposed to be comparatively well, because they were well enough to be moved. Johannes wondered how badly wounded soldiers had to be if they couldn't be moved.

He was relieved when the convoy of ambulances pulled up outside a huge old house in the middle of the countryside, and someone said that they had reached their destination. The soldiers made signs to offer the children something to eat, but only Kathrin felt like eating, so she trotted off to the kitchens of the big house, and came back half an hour later, with an extra cold sausage and an apple for Johannes.

He still couldn't eat. He had been longing to get out of the jerking, jolting hot ambulance which smelt of sickness, but as soon as he got out, all he could do was to sit down on the grass with his back against a tree, and then lie down because he was too sick to sit up straight. They had told him the ambulances would stop about 100 miles north-west of Stuttgart, but he had no idea how far that was. He didn't want to think of how they would get to Stuttgart now.

The only thing he could think of, and he tried to banish that thought from his mind as well, was Frau von Kempner, dead in the garden. Should he have buried her? Who had buried her? His mother had said she was sure that all the people killed in the bombings were given a decent Christian burial . . . Was his mother really dead? Frau von Kempner . . . He felt sick again and then he fainted.

Kathrin was sitting by him holding his hand when he woke up, still quite calm about what was happening. She was hardly ever afraid.

She looked up and smiled at a soldier who was walking over to get something from one of the ambulances. "Hallo little one" he said, "what're you doing round here? You'd better run along home now." She smiled at him, showing her bright white teeth, but she hadn't understood a word he said. "Hey, which of you speaks German round here?" he shouted to some of the other soldiers hanging around in the courtyard in front of the old manor house which served as a hospital.

A young soldier, a doctor, came over and spoke to them in perfect, accent-free German. "What are you two youngsters doing here?" he asked. "Do you come from the village?"

No one knew where the children had come from. As usual, the soldiers who had brought them all the way from Berlin had disappeared. They were far too busy with the patients from their ambulances to bother about a couple of children who had been dumped on them by the officer at the station.

"We're from Berlin," Kathrin explained, "and we're going to Onkel Otto." She smiled at the doctor. "And where's Onkel Otto?" The doctor spoke this time to Johannes, who, with his eyes open, was staring up at the fresh green shoots of a horse-chestnut tree, brushing the sky with colour. Kathrin answered for him, "He's with Tante Edith in Stuttgart." The doctor looked seriously at Johannes, "Can't your brother hear me?", and this time Kathrin didn't answer. This time even she was frightened as she looked at Johannes and saw his passive face, his eyes empty of any response.

Then, "I think he's very tired," she said, "poor Hannes." "Then we'd better give you both a bed for the night," said the doctor, and carried Johannes, a small, thin bony creature, as if he were a doll, into the house.

"His arm hurts," said Kathrin, when the nurse had given them two mattresses to sleep on, so the doctor had to be sent for again. He checked the elbow, wrist and fingers. "Nothing broken," he said, "nothing but a severe contusion. You'll just have to wait for the pain to go away youngster," he said, "Hasn't got a temperature, has he?" he asked the nurse. She shook her head. "Then the sister must be right." He patted Kathrin's blond curls. "It must be just extreme tiredness. Either that, or he's seen something that shocked him very much. You'd better get some sleep now. And see if you can get him to eat something in the morning," he said to the nurse.

They didn't leave the hospital for another four days. On the first two days, Johannes simply didn't make the effort to get out of bed. He just stared at the wood-panelled wall of the former dining room where they had been put with ten other patients, and scarcely responded when people spoke to him. But even on the third day, though Johannes insisted all of a sudden that his arm felt a good deal better, and that they'd better set off as soon as possible, the nurse wouldn't let them go, because Johannes still hadn't eaten anything.

On the fourth day she made a bargain with them that if Johannes ate three good hospital meals the next day she would let them go. She had a good way of keeping them there too. When they had arrived, she had offered to look after their pram for them and had locked it up safely in her store cupboard, and she would only let them have it again when she thought they were fit to travel.

And they had to convince her that they knew where they were going. It was up to Kathrin to gain their release by insisting that she would look after Johannes. Though his arm was getting better every day he didn't seem to have any strength left. He seemed to have lost the will to do anything for himself.

But the nurse had her work cut out with the new patients who were arriving every day. It wasn't part of her job to look after the homeless orphans who were tramping round Germany in those chaotic days after the war had ended. The only thing she could do for Johannes was to take his stitches out and wish them both good luck in the morning as they set out.

Kathrin had begun to understand some of the things the nurse had babbled on to them in Russian, so, as they pushed their pram away down the hospital drive, she waved and smiled and shouted back to the nurse, "You feel better!"

Johannes, still depressed and tired, had paid scant attention to what the nurse said. He understood from the tone of her voice and her smiling face that she was always cheerful. But her cheerfulness was more difficult for him to understand than anything she had tried to say to him in the Russian language.

17

It took Johannes and Kathrin a good deal more than two weeks to get to the outskirts of Stuttgart—on foot—weeks in which they had almost nothing to eat, so that when they finally reached their destination their feet were swollen, not from the walking, but from the beginnings of a slow starvation which would, that winter, claim the lives of thousands who had managed to struggle through the war relatively unhurt.

Sometimes they were lucky; in exchange for a pair of gold earrings from the brown bag, a farmer's wife gave them a few carrots. An old lady in one of the villages they tramped through ran after them and gave them both milk to drink, and wouldn't take anything in payment. But in other places no one had anything to spare, even when they offered to pay.

They weren't the only ones on the move at that terrible time when Germany had just been defeated. The roads from east to west were full of refugees, fleeing because they were afraid of the Russians. Men, women and children tramped along. Some were pushing large hand-carts, with the few precious possessions they had been able to salvage from the bombings—a clock, books, sometimes even an armchair. Some were carrying only a rucksack and the clothes they had fled in.

If the peasants in the villages they passed through had offered food to the two dirty, tired-looking, skinny children pushing a doll's pram, they would have had to offer it to everyone, and they had little enough food for themselves and their families.

And there was another reason why the people in the

villages they came to refused to open their doors to them, or sent them packing without any food. At that time, when the war was over, but the after-effects of war were still hovering around like vultures ready to swoop on any creature as soon as it appeared to be dead, many of the children who found themselves totally alone and homeless, without food or hope, were forming up into gangs to steal the food they needed for survival—by force, if necessary.

So the emotions which greeted two children, however small, tramping through the country on their own were far more likely to be fear and hatred than kindness or pity.

Often Johannes and Kathrin got lost. There were no maps and few road signs, so they were completely dependent on people telling them the way. The directions they received often turned out to be the wrong ones because people were so anxious to get away from them, to get rid of them. In those days, stray children were treated rather as we would treat stray dogs. At best, we give them a wide berth—in case they've got fleas or expect us to feed them. At worst we shout at them or throw stones at them to frighten them off, because we fear they will bite us.

The children slept out in the open, grateful that the nights were becoming warmer, and so exhausted at the end of each day that they were oblivious to whether their bed was a prickling pile of old hay in a barn or just a grass verge. Only in the mornings did they notice how stiff and uncomfortable they felt. And one morning they woke up to find that their pram and all its contents had been stolen.

When everything seemed hopeless and Kathrin cried from hunger and exhaustion, Johannes still trudged on and made her do the same. The only thing they could do was to keep going, keep on walking. He knew it would be fatal to stop before they reached Stuttgart. They had to keep going.

He had reached a kind of a wall when they had arrived at

the military hospital, when despair had overcome him and he had wanted only to give up the struggle to live, to fall quietly asleep and never wake up any more. But after resting there, he was strong enough to see that they had to climb over any obstacles they came to, no matter how long it took them. He could see that it would get even harder. But as they couldn't go back to Berlin the only thing left was to fight on till they got to Stuttgart.

They experienced a momentary elation when they reached the outskirts of Stuttgart. Johannes even knew the name of the street in the centre where Onkel Otto and Tante Edith had lived. But he had no idea whether they were still living there, whether they and their house had survived at all. And as they plodded downhill on the winding roads towards the valley which was the centre of Stuttgart, Johannes' courage nearly failed him once again.

The whole of the centre, and the houses which had formerly stood on the slopes rising away from the centre, were stripped to the bare bones, like a skeleton, but like a blackened, charred skeleton, with flimsy, burnt bits of clothing, still hanging in shreds from it. What Johannes saw was a forest of grotesque trees such as he had seen in Berlin, pain-twisted branches, stripped bare of any leaves, even though it was high summer. Kathrin saw only the great mounds of stone and rubble piled everywhere, with so many lives buried underneath. For most of the time they walked down the middle of the streets where there were fewer boulders and bricks for Kathrin's little legs to stumble over.

Onkel Otto's house was an empty, burnt-out, roofless shell, the windows like sightless eyes. The children weren't at all surprised. They would have been much more surprised to find it still intact after the ruins they had already passed by.

"Are you looking for someone?" screeched a woman

115

who had emerged from a cellar entrance across the way, while they stood staring at the ruins. Johannes gave her Onkel Otto's name. "Oh, they don't live here any more," she said stupidly. Johannes wanted to hit her for being such a stupid busybody.

"They were still here January, I think," she went on, coming over to them. "That's when our house was hit too. We live in the cellar now, but it's not too bad. You get used to it. He lost his eye, you know." She nodded over to where Onkel Otto's house had been. "That's why he was home on leave when they were bombed out.

"But none of them was hurt, as far as I know. I don't know where they've gone to, though. Now, hadn't you better run along home? This is no place for a child to be hanging about, you know. They're dangerous, these ruins. Could fall on you at any minute." Neither of the children made any move to go.

She peered more closely at them, shading her eyes against the sun. "Are you hungry?" she asked. Both of them nodded. "Look, you can come down into my place and have a bit of bread, if you want. We've not much else, but you can both have one piece of bread." They went with her. Frau Krüger, her name was.

She lived in a one-roomed cellar with her old mother, who had her bed down in the cellar, because she had had it taken down there after the air raids began. The old woman couldn't see very well and she had no teeth, but she said they were welcome. "Sit down, little sparrows that you are, skinny, dirty little sparrows. Sit down."

She moved her legs a fraction, so they could sit on the edge of her bed. "You'll have to give them a wash, Anna," she said sharply to her daughter. "The boy smells. Give him a nice, hot bath." "There's no bath here, mother," said Frau Krüger patiently. "I'll take them out to the pipe down the street afterwards to see if there's any water."

"I'm sure the little girl would like some sweets, Anna," said the old woman after a while. "Give her some of those from the blue tin with gold writing on—over there on the mantelpiece." Kathrin's eyes lit up, but Frau Krüger shook her head. "We haven't had any sweets for years," she said, "not since the first year of the war." Laughing, she pointed to her head and said, "She's not so good up here any more. Well, what can you expect at 82? But she's no trouble. Good as gold she is. Now, here's your bread."

The children ate very slowly, Johannes with his eyes closed, savouring every crumb. They cupped their hands tightly around the bread, to make sure that not a single crumb fell to the floor. It was dry, old bread, so it didn't crumble very much. Frau Krüger just sat and stared at them as they ate, painfully slowly, chewing every mouthful till it disintegrated. She shook her head again and again. "Poor little starving sparrows," was all she could think of to say.

Then, when they had finished eating, "Look, you can stay here for a day or two, if you like—till you find whoever it is you're looking for. That's if you don't mind sleeping on the floor. Mother and I use the bed. But we'll have to go to the Red Cross or to the soldiers to see if we can find you some food, and perhaps they'll know how we can find your uncle."

"I know what you must do, Anna" ordered the old woman from her bed. "You must take those children to the Red Cross. The Red Cross finds people when they're lost. They found my son after the last war, you know," she said to the children, and then she lowered her voice. "His wife wouldn't have him back, you know. Said he'd been going round with all them French women." "Sh! mother," said Frau Krüger, "they don't want to hear that kind of thing."

At the Red Cross station in the centre of Stuttgart, they said they would see if they could help the children to find their parents, or at least some relatives, as their parents were probably dead. But the woman they saw there said that meant they would have to stay in the Red Cross children's camp. "We can't have you living with complete strangers," she said.

"I'm sorry, Frau Krüger. I don't mean to be offensive, but in some cases, when the parents have been found, we've then discovered that the children have disappeared again. The family they had been staying with just upped and left without leaving any address behind at all. And then we have to start searching all over again."

A doctor examined them first. In Johannes' medical record he wrote, "Johannes S.—Water on the knee and ankle joints, bones sticking out like a skeleton on the shoulders and chest, lice and scabies." Kathrin's medical report was a little better. Johannes had always been thin, even when they were living with Frau von Kempner, and his sickness hadn't helped, whereas Kathrin had been a little fatter at the time when Herr von Kempner was executed and their food first began to get really scarce. The only things the doctor could prescribe for them at first were just what Frau Krüger's mother had thought of—a good wash and careful feeding. Johannes was examined and scrubbed by a bully of a nurse several times a day, but they were given enough to eat for the first time in months—never very much, but at least something.

One day, a man came and took photographs of them and other children in the camp, and the photographs appeared on a poster, entitled "Lost Children Looking For Their Parents". There were other, similar posters which Johannes used to study avidly. These ones had the heading, "Parents Looking For Their Lost Children".

He never found any sign of his parents, but one day, at the end of September, Onkel Otto turned up at the refugee camp, and took them home with him.

Home was a one-roomed flat, with a kitchen and toilet shared with three other families, in a big old house just next to the building where the American soldiers had their headquarters. In that one, large room Onkel Otto and Tante Edith slept with their five children, but Onkel Otto had rushed off to fetch Johannes and Kathrin as soon as he saw the poster with their names on it.

He insisted that they had enough room for them, and the people at the Red Cross didn't question him very closely about how much room he had, as long as he was able to prove he was a relative. So at long last Johannes and Kathrin were home, with people who cared about them and hugged them and wanted to know, if they went out, where they were going to and when they would be coming back. Johannes could begin to learn again what it meant to be cheerful.

Onkel Otto was nearly always cheerful. He was lucky too. Admittedly, he had lost his left eye, but that had meant he was sent home from the fighting. "It could have been worse," he told anyone who sympathised with him, "I could have lost one of my children instead." A lot of the people listening to him when he talked like that thought that this wouldn't have been such a bad thing, as he then wouldn't have had so many mouths to feed—let alone the two new children he had taken in.

But Onkel Otto would have told them he was lucky in that respect too. Immediately after the war he had been taken on as a cook by the Americans, because he had worked as a chef in one of Stuttgart's biggest hotels before the war. So he was often allowed to bring left-overs home for his family. As far as food was concerned, they didn't have anything like the hard time other families had, the ones who had to trudge miles out into the countryside taking a precious antique clock or jewellery which they hoped to exchange for an even more precious sack of potatoes. Sometimes people tried to go by train to relatives in the country, to beg or barter for things to eat, but there were almost no passenger trains, so it was a very common sight to see people hitching a ride, perched on top of swaying goods trains. At every station they would be chased off by soldiers or railwaymen, but they usually found a way of climbing back on again just when the train was puffing on its way out of the station.

The main thing Johannes' family were short of was any way of heating their flat in that bitterly cold winter. Every day, Johannes and his cousins went down near the railway tracks, to see how much coal they could collect for the oven, by picking up the bits which had fallen off the goods trains. It was never very much, because they weren't the only ones with that idea.

Sometimes they found wood from bombed-out houses, but that fuel supply soon ran out. When people got too cold, there were public warming places, in stations or halls, where a stove was set up in the middle of the room and people could crowd in and get warm, at least for a few minutes of the day.

Onkel Otto didn't smoke. But every day, on his way to the improvised school set up in a former cinema, Johannes saw the misery of the people who did smoke, when cigarettes were almost impossible to get hold of. As he passed by the American barracks, he saw men and women, young as well as old, bent almost double, with their eyes skimming the ground. They were the ones who had discovered that you could make one new cigarette out of seven cigarette ends, and that the best place to find cigarette ends was in front of any American barracks, where the soldiers had thrown them away.

One December day near Christmas, as Johannes stopped outside the barracks to watch an old man picking cigarette ends up from the icy ground, he felt someone pulling at the hood of his duffle coat. It was an American soldier, smiling at him. "You'd better run along home, youngster," he said. "Don't hang around here in the cold."

Johannes set off again, running the last short stretch to their house, and then realised that there was something heavy in the hood of his coat. It was a large bar of chocolate.

Johannes had never tasted chocolate in his whole life. He sat down on the stone-cold steps up to the front door of their house and looked at it for a long time. It had red paper on top and silver paper under that. His fingers tingled, with excitement rather than cold. He was ten years old and he had never seen a bar of chocolate, but he knew what it was all right, in spite of the English writing.

And he knew it was something good, something magical, because of the way his elder cousin Peter spoke about it. He was fourteen and had eaten the most amazing things—oranges, bananas, dates, and even chocolate, when he was small. What should he do?

Johannes' first thought was to hide the chocolate in the small rucksack he took to school, and not to tell anyone else about it. He would eat a tiny piece every day—or perhaps every other day, and then it would last him a good long time. He could feel with his fingers through the wrapping paper; there were ten squares of chocolate.

But then he had a better idea. He hid the chocolate inside his rucksack before going into the house and then stowed his rucksack, more carefully than usual, under the bed where he slept with three of his cousins, Erik, Harald and Günter. Erik was the same age as Johannes, Harald and Günter were eight and six, and the youngest cousin, Liesl, was four. Peter had a bed all to himself, and Liesl and Kathrin slept on a mattress beside Onkel Otto and Tante Edith's bed, which was rolled up and pushed underneath the bed during the daytime.

They were so lucky, Onkel Otto said frequently to Tante Edith, and then always added, "It could have been much worse. We might have had to make do with a damp cellar, with no beds at all—in this weather. We're one of the luckiest families on earth this Christmas." And he would take on his knee anyone who happened to be around and give them a great big hug, to show them how lucky he felt himself to be.

A few days before Christmas Eve, everything was in chaos. No one could find anything—especially their toys. But on Christmas Eve itself they were determined to celebrate Christmas as well as they could. First they all went to church—in the cinema where Johannes and his cousins usually went to school. Nearly all the proper churches in Stuttgart had been totally demolished. Lots of people were crying as the priest conducted the service and talked, as he did every year, about how Mary and Joseph had had nowhere to lay their head when they arrived in Bethlehem.

But Onkel Otto's one eye was twinkling with laughter when the service was over, and he shook hands with everyone, with the kind of hearty handshake which makes people have to hold on a bit longer so they don't fall over. He wished everyone, including the priest, "Merry Christmas" and, telling them all that he'd managed to get hold of a bottle of cognac, invited them to drop in if they wanted to be filled with the Holy Spirit on Christmas Day.

At home, there was no Christmas tree. "Can't get one for love nor money," said Onkel Otto, and produced a piece of mistletoe. "This is what the Americans have," he said. "Everyone has to give me a kiss when I hold it over my head." After this ceremony had been taken care of, with as many repeat performances as tyrannical Onkel Otto cared to demand, Tante Edith produced a candle and lit it, and they sang all the old Christmas songs.

When they sang "Silent Night" it was Tante Edith's turn to cry, with her arms round Harald and Johannes. "Hey, there's no need for crying, little one," said Onkel Otto. He was an enormous man and he used to lift Tante Edith up and throw her around like one of the children. "No need for that. We've got every reason to be happy and grateful."

"I'm crying because I'm happy," she said, and then, "but Kathrin looks so like her mother." "And Johannes is the spitting image of his father," said Onkel Otto, "but that's no reason for crying. We'll be lucky if they're as like them when they get older. Then they'll do us proud, and their parents. God rest their souls." "Amen," said Tante Edith.

Onkel Otto looked very solemn, and stared round with his one eye at all the children looking solemnly back at him. "Come on," he said, "this is no time to be sad. Everyone down on your knees and look under your beds! That's an order!"

They all knelt down, and drew out the treasures from underneath their beds. Kathrin and Liesl's dolls, which had mysteriously disappeared in the week before Christmas re-emerged, brushed, combed and dressed in the brand-new clothes which Tante Edith had sewn for them. Günter and Harald found their missing fire-engines totally transformed by a new coat of paint, Erik was given a book, Peter a torch and Tante Edith a pair of stockings.

Johannes had a book too, a nearly new one, but without his glasses he could only read if he held the book right up close to his nose. At that time he literally did always have his nose in a book.

"Where on earth did you get these from?" gasped Tante Edith, holding up the stockings. She had asked the same question before when Onkel Otto had secretly brought home the books and the torch, and now she received the same answer. "Oh, you just have to know the right people to go and see, and you can get hold of most things," said Onkel Otto, and his shoulders shook with silent laughter at the pleasure he had brought.

Johannes dragged his rucksack out from under the bed, "I've got something for you all too," he said, blinking at them in his short-sighted way. "Close your eyes." He pulled out the chocolate and put it behind his back. "Now you can open them." They all opened their eyes. "Oh, Hannes, what is it?" asked Liesl, exasperated. Johannes looked all round, to make sure he had everyone's full attention and then, slowly, reverently, he brought the chocolate from behind his back and held it up for everyone to see.

A loud "Oooh!" went round the room, and then there was silence. He was like the magician who has just pulled a rabbit out of a hat. He had them spellbound.

He passed the chocolate round in its paper first, for everyone to see, and there was no fighting over it. Everyone handed it on carefully to his neighbour as if it were a precious piece of china. Then it came back to Johannes.

"Shall we eat it today?" He looked hesitantly at Onkel Otto. "Up to you, lad. I can't think of any better time, can you?" It was the best chocolate Johannes ever tasted.

18

Two important things happened the following year, 1946. The first was that Johannes finally got some new glasses. His teacher had kept on insisting that he needed them and Johannes, who couldn't be kept away from books, had kept on reading, with the book perched on the end of his nose, and had made his eyes even worse. So Onkel Otto had finally managed to get some glasses for him, through the American army doctor.

The second most important thing was their move out to Möhringen, a suburb of Stuttgart, where they lived in a house with two flats in it. Theirs was the upstairs flat and had two bedrooms. They even had a large section of the garden, where there were two cherry trees and where they could grow vegetables.

Onkel Otto carried on working for the Americans, but the children went to different schools—Johannes, Peter and Erik to a secondary school in Stuttgart, and the younger ones to the local primary school.

Tante Edith worked in Stuttgart too, helping to clear up the ruins which still covered the city. Building materials for new houses were in very short supply, so thousands of people like Tante Edith worked in the ruins, scraping old mortar off the bricks from bombed-out buildings so that they were fit to be used again. On school holidays, or in the afternoons when there was no school, the children helped too. No one rested. Everyone felt it was their duty to help to re-build the city, so everyone who didn't have some other important job helped with clearing up and re-building. The city had reached rock-bottom, and things could only get better—if everybody worked.

On 23rd May 1949, when Johannes was nearly fourteen, he was helping Onkel Otto and Peter out in the garden at about five o'clock when Kathrin and Liesl came running round from the front of the house where they had been playing.

"Papi, Papi!" they shouted. "There's a funny, smelly old man standing there staring at our house." "He's dirty, and I'm frightened of him, Papi," added Kathrin. "We're not going to play at the front any more." Kathrin thought of her uncle and aunt as parents now. Only Johannes continued to call them Onkel and Tante.

Onkel Otto was furious with the girls. They rarely saw him so angry. "Stop that nonsense," he said, stabbing his spade into the ground. Then he bent down and put his arms round both of the girls. "You mustn't say horrible things like that about people who aren't as lucky as we are. That man out there at the front probably hasn't got anywhere to go.

"There's still hundreds like him who've lost their homes and their families and don't know where to turn, so they just have to tramp the roads, sleeping in barns or wherever they can find a place. How can you expect them to be clean? We've got to help people like him, not send him away like a dirty, mangy dog."

They all went upstairs to the kitchen to see what there was to give to the man. Tante Edith said she'd noticed him already the day before, leaning against the wall staring at the house. "Poor, desolate, God-forsaken creature," she said, "I didn't have anything to spare for him yesterday, but now there's some bread and sausage you can take out to him. Have you got a glass of beer as well?" Onkel Otto had.

He wanted Kathrin and Liesl to take the food down to the strange man, but they were still too frightened, so Tante Edith said, "Leave them. I'll take it down myself."

Onkel Otto went with her, carrying the beer. Kathrin and Liesl went with them as far as the garden door.

Johannes was left alone in the kitchen, and he was able to look down at the man from behind the curtains. Very, very old he looked, and he was wearing an enormous, heavy, grey overcoat, in spite of the warm May sunshine, and a strange peaked cap trimmed with fur, with flaps that could be pulled down over his ears. His face was thin, with the bones sticking out, and there was a grey stubble on his chin where he hadn't shaved for some time. He stared sadly at the house, with eyes which looked enormous in his bony face.

Onkel Otto and Tante Edith got to the gate of the front garden and offered him the food, but he didn't sit down on the wall and eat gratefully, as Johannes had seen other tramps doing before him.

For what seemed an age, he talked to Tante Edith and Onkel Otto, all of them looking very serious, and then suddenly Tante Edith, putting the food down on the wall, threw her arms round the strange man's neck and kissed him, and Onkel Otto grabbed hold of the man's hand and shook it over and over and over again, and then almost dragged him towards the house.

And Johannes knew that his father had come back to them.

CATCH A KELPIE

If you enjoyed this book
you would probably enjoy our other Kelpies.

Here's a complete list to choose from: